THE COLLECTORS

Karma Police Book Three

SEAN PLATT

DAVID W. WRIGHT

STERLING & STONE

THE COLLECTORS

Prologue

I wake up in a chaos of light, sound, and movement.

Someone is violently shaking me.

A man's voice, commanding: "Chelsea, Chelsea, wake up!"

I open my eyes, gasping for air in shallow hitches, desperately attempting to fill my lungs with air.

My eyes are blurry, my burning throat is sour with vomit, and my face is sticky with sickness. My head feels like someone's been at it with a hammer.

I can barely keep my eyes open or focus on the man's face. I turn, frantically searching for something to help me catch my breath. I see others in the room, a woman and a teenage boy standing over the bed, staring down at me, concerned, scared.

While I'm not pulling in any of Chelsea's memories, I can piece together that this is her family, and they're trying to save her.

What happened?

Her mother is clutching the phone and half yelling into it. "She's awake, but she doesn't look good. Please, hurry."

My heart is racing, head swimming as I continue to gasp, unable to properly breathe.

What the hell is happening?

Chelsea's father sits me up, maybe trying to help clear my throat.

Our eyes meet, and for a moment I can focus enough to note his palpable fear, the fear and love of a parent powerless to save his child.

Just when I think I might be catching my breath, everything goes black.

Chapter One

I WAKE to the sound of chimes coming through a speaker.

I reach out, fumble with the unfamiliar phone, find a way to kill the alarm.

The phone's calendar tells me it's Tuesday morning, meaning I've missed an entire day since waking up late Sunday evening/early Monday morning as Chelsea. I'm not sure where I go when my host sleeps, passes out, or dies. It's as if I cease to exist until I rise in another body. Do I sleep when they do? If so, what part of me is sleeping? It's not as if I have a physical body — that I know of — which needs rest.

Can a soul sleep?

I sit up, wondering how I can learn what happened to Chelsea. I don't even know her last name, so it's not like I can search on the Internet. But as I catch my reflection in the mirror above the dresser, I realize that I won't need to search far.

I've woken as Chelsea's brother, high school freshman, Billy Caldwell. As his brain fills me in, I'm surprised to learn that his father is famous, a Christian self-help author named Jack Caldwell, esteemed for, among other things, books on raising children who won't succumb to today's many evils.

Hmm, wonder how he's *taking this.*

Billy's brain fills me in on a few other things, chief among them: Chelsea is still alive, lying in a coma in the hospital. Billy's mom, Susan, is staying with Chelsea while Dad stays home to look after Billy. I also know that Chelsea left a suicide note. It simply said:

I'm sorry I let you down.

I'm startled by three sharp raps on the door.

Billy's father opens it, already dressed in a handsome suit.

"Come on, champ. I've got a meeting. I need to drop you off early."

"Okay," I say, getting out of bed. Billy's body is tired, likely exhausted from the previous day's emotional turmoil. I'm surprised his father is sending him to school just one day after his sister tried killing herself, but as Billy's memories surge forth, I see that Jack Caldwell expects a lot from his children. While Billy *did* stay home yesterday, there was never any question that he'd be back at school today.

I look around the room. I've woken in at least a dozen teenage boys' rooms since I've been body jumping, and Billy's is, by far, the neatest. Hell, it's neater than nearly anywhere I've woken: designed with an OCD-like compulsion towards sparsity and cleanliness. The perfectly organized walk-in closet looks like a shrine to orderliness, filled with mostly look-alike school uniforms: pressed khakis, starched shirts, six pairs of identical polished black shoes.

I get dressed, run some water through Billy's thick blond hair, and brush it back. As I stare at my reflection, I wonder why I've woken in this body. Am I being given a chance to save Chelsea, or am I expected to kill someone?

~

Billy's father doesn't say a word on the way to school. At least not to me. Instead, he's on the phone with his agent, Waylon Carter, discussing "the situation" with Chelsea.

From what I can gather, nobody has figured out why she tried to kill herself or what she was apologizing for in her suicide note. And I don't think Jack told the police anything about the note. I get the feeling that this was at Waylon's suggestion, though I'm not quite sure why, since most of their conversation is almost in code, Jack not wanting to say too much in front of me.

I wonder what he's hiding. Does he know what Chelsea was apologizing for? Am I here to find out?

Jack stops the car in front St. Paul's Academy. The posh-looking school seems more like a college campus than any high school I've been in, with a large brick main building with stone pillars, a spacious courtyard with trees, walkways, and fountains where kids are already hanging out before the morning bell. Another three smaller buildings are pocked around the courtyard, and at the far edge of the sprawling campus looms a large and admittedly gorgeous cathedral.

Jack tells Waylon to hold on. Then he leans over, plants a kiss on my forehead, and says, "Have a good day, Billy."

"You too," I say, slipping out of the midnight-blue Porsche Panamera.

I watch Billy's father drive away, off to do whatever it is he's doing to take care of "the situation." I wonder if he's at all afraid that his daughter might die. I sure couldn't tell from his call. It was mostly about getting to the bottom of what happened, finding out and controlling the information before it leaked. Maybe he's afraid a suicide attempt will ruin his reputation as a good Christian parent who tells other people how to raise their kids.

Billy's memories of his father are fuzzy. I get the impression that he's a good man, but extremely busy. But not by any neglectful levels. He still makes time for the important things — like Billy's tennis tournament last summer.

I wander the campus, waiting for Billy's memories to give me direction. School doesn't start for another forty minutes, and I'm not even sure which class he has first.

I sit down on the fountain's edge and stare at the coins along the bottom.

I dig into my pockets, but can't find any change to buy a wish.

Figures.

I search Billy's backpack, find his iPad, pull it out, and peruse his books. I smile in recognition of a few authors I recall: Ray Bradbury, Stephen King, and Phillip K. Dick. I remember some of the stories I've read and feel some nostalgia looking over the titles. But then that feeling is replaced with a hollow sorrow as I realize the memories I have of these books aren't *mine* — I have none of my own — but instead belong to my previous hosts.

Maybe I can read a bit before school starts and make my own memories.

I pick a book by Stephen King and Peter Straub — *The Talisman* — and click on it. It opens to the first page, meaning that either Billy hasn't read it yet, or he's already finished and the book has reset to the starting point. I'm not familiar enough with iPads or the various reading apps to know. I start reading the tale of Jack Sawyer.

About ten minutes in, the story is broken by a girl's voice. "Billy?"

I look up to see two girls, a blonde and a redhead, approaching me, both wearing matching uniforms — blue dresses and white shirts — but they somehow manage to find a way to express themselves. The blonde is wearing a floral headband, beaded with tiny silk flowers and matching rosebud earrings; the redhead has a scarf that looks like it probably belongs to her mother, even though she owns the look. Both of their backpacks are plastered with buttons.

I'm drawing a blank on their names.

Shit.

"Hey," the blonde says, "how's your sister doing?"

Are they Chelsea's friends? They do look *a bit* older than freshmen. I'm not sure how to answer. I don't want to give out any private information, or make "the situation" any worse than it is for Dear Ol' Dad.

The redhead says, "I'm surprised you're even here today."

I nod. "Yeah, me too."

"How's Chelsea?" the blonde asks again. There's something about her piercing blue eyes that I don't like — an iciness inside them.

I try to shake my suspicions and give the best possible answer. "She's still in the hospital. Hanging in there."

"We're so sorry," the redhead says. She seems slightly more sincere than the blonde.

"What did you hear?" I say. "I mean, how much is out there?"

The girls trade an uncertain glance. Then the redhead opens her mouth. "Well, we heard she's in a coma. But … "

"What?" I ask.

The blonde says, "Well, some people are saying she tried to kill herself."

She says it almost as if looking for confirmation, so she can be among the First To Know.

She stares at me, but I don't confirm or deny. "Well, people love to talk about stuff they don't know."

"So, it isn't true?" the redhead asks.

"We don't know what happened, but we're hoping for the best." I figure that's the safest thing I can say for both Chelsea's privacy, and for Billy's standing at school whenever he returns to his body.

The blonde doesn't seem to like this response. She gives me a fake little smile, leans forward, puts her hand on my shoulder, and makes her eyes overly large and artificially sad. "Well, I hope she feels better."

But I don't believe a word.

The girls leave, and I decide to find another spot before more people I don't know approach me.

I find a spot behind the library and am just about to dive back into my book when I hear a male British accent.

"Billy?"

I look up to see a friendly face, Pete Arber, who I recognize as Billy's best friend since sixth grade.

Pete has long brown hair with blue and red highlights. He's fiercely flamboyant and very open about his bisexuality. This makes him someone that Jack Caldwell doesn't approve of. He hasn't quite forbidden Billy from being friends with him, but he has threatened it enough times that Billy's afraid of the eventual day when Pete does something that Jack doesn't approve of.

"*What* are you doing here?" Pete sits beside me and puts a hand to his mouth before I can answer. "Seriously? Your dad *made* you come to school *today?*"

"It's okay. It's better than sitting at home not being able to do anything."

"You could be at the hospital, with your mom!"

"Yeah, well I guess Dad felt school was more important."

"What a cunt."

I laugh.

Pete laughs, too.

"So, how is she? Any word?"

I have a flash of Billy texting Pete yesterday from the hospital, updating him. I don't *think* anything has changed since then.

"Nothing new."

"Shit, that sucks. I'm sorry."

I stare out at the courtyard, watching kids hanging out, throwing footballs and Frisbees, carefree, laughing, going about their lives oblivious, or blind to, Billy's suffering.

"It's okay. She'll get better," I say, not sure if I'm trying to convince myself or Pete.

We sit in silence for a moment. I feel uneasy because while Billy and Pete are best friends, I don't have enough of their shared history to turn an awkward quiet into something comfortable. I feel a need to fill the air with something, but don't know what to say. So I opt for silence instead.

Pete is fidgeting, sitting cross-legged and bouncing his knees like he wants to say something.

"What is it?" I ask.

"I don't know if I should say anything."

"What?" I ask, leaning forward.

He folds his hands, covers his mouth with a deep, dramatic sigh, and finally meets my eyes.

"*What?*" I ask again.

"You've got to promise that you won't do anything crazy."

"What is it?"

"Promise first."

I promise.

"You know how people have been calling your sister a slut the past couple of weeks, but we didn't know why?"

I nod, even though Billy's memories haven't filled me in on this yet.

"Have you heard anything about a video?"

"Video? What video?"

"That your sister was in?"

"No."

"Shit." He runs his hands through his hair. "I didn't think so."

"What video?"

"You've got to promise that you won't do anything stupid."

"I already did."

"And promise not to be mad at me."

"Why would I be mad at you?"

"For not showing you sooner."

"Showing me *what?*"

He reaches into his pants pocket, pulls out his phone, flips through some screens, then holds it to his chest, meeting my eyes.

"You promise?"

"Yes!" I say, grabbing the phone.

I look down at the screen and see that the video is titled, *high school cam slut spreads for me.*

My heart racing anxiously, I press play.

The video shows Chelsea sitting in front of a webcam in a dark room. She's wearing a light gray tee, hair pulled back in a ponytail. She looks uncomfortable. There's no audio, but I can tell she's typing something.

I look up at Pete. "What is this?"

"Keep watching," he says, looking away as if he can't stand to see me watching it.

Chelsea takes off her shirt.

She's sitting there in her bra, staring at the screen, but there's nothing seductive about this. Her eyes are wet like she's holding back tears or had just finished crying. Her lips are quivering. Her jaw is sticking out, almost, but not quite, defiantly.

My stomach feels like I'm in a jostled boat.

What the hell is this?

Chelsea shakes her head.

A long pause where she watches the screen. Someone must be giving her instructions. Maybe that's why there's no audio; whoever recorded this deleted their part in this sick little film.

She wipes her eyes then takes off her bra. She starts fast but stops halfway as if instructed to go slower, to be more playful.

She slows down, removing it more teasingly, then reveals her breasts.

Another long pause.

Another head shake.

Then she plays with her nipples.

The sickness in my stomach grows. I don't want to see any more. But at the same time, I feel like I have to — I need to see what happened to Billy's sister.

After history's longest minute, the camera pans down. As Chelsea removes her shorts, I return the phone to Pete.

"I can't watch any more. What the hell is this? And where did it come from?"

Pete takes the phone and slips it back into his pants pocket as if he's ashamed to own it.

"Someone uploaded it to a porn site a couple of weeks ago. Kids started sharing it. A few even posted it onto her Facebook page, along with nasty messages calling your sister a slut and stuff, before she removed her page."

"A couple of weeks ago? And you're just telling me now?"

"I didn't find out about it until last week, and what was I supposed to say, 'Yo, I saw your sister in a porn video?'"

"It's *not* a porn video! Someone obviously made her do this. You can tell by her expression. Does it look like she's enjoying it?"

"Hey, believe me, Billy, I'm the last person to judge! And even if she *was* enjoying it, even if she sent this to a boyfriend and was 100 percent compliant, that doesn't give anyone the right to post it on a porn site, or any of these fuckers the right to judge her."

"We've gotta get this taken down! She's a teenager for God's sake!"

"She's eighteen. And dude, the Internet is forever. Even if you take it down at this site, the person who did it, or hell, anyone who downloaded it, can upload it to a thousand more sites just like it."

Is this *why she tried to kill herself?*

"Fuck!" I stare at the ground, feeling rage, frustration, and helplessness pounding through me.

"Wait a second," I say, Billy's memories filling in a few details. "Chelsea didn't have a boyfriend. I mean, she's never had a boyfriend. So, who do you think she recorded this for?"

"Maybe she had a boyfriend we don't know about? Hell, if it happened before she turned eighteen, maybe we *can* get it taken down, at least from the most popular porn sites."

"I think I'd know if my sister had a boyfriend."

"I dunno. With your dad being like he is, I can see her not wanting to tell anyone."

"But she knows I wouldn't judge her or tell anyone. We get along."

"I dunno." Pete's eyes widen, and he looks at me.

"What?"

"I might be able to find out who did this."

"How?"

"Just let me work my contacts," he says with a glint in his eyes. Pete enjoys playing detective almost as much as he loves gossip. If anyone in school can find out who's behind this, it's Billy's best friend. "I'll see what I come up with and get back to you at lunch."

~

THE NEXT FEW hours are hell.

Kids coming up to me with false consolation, asking questions about Chelsea's welfare, some even asking if she left a note. I don't trust any of them.

How many of those same kids were laughing at her, calling my sister a slut behind her back? How many of them shared this video? How many of these so-called friends are only pretenders? How many are to blame for her suicide attempt?

I hate them all, though I know it isn't fair. I can't tell sincerity from charade with these private school kids. They're all so damn good at living behind a facade.

I spend Billy's class time trying to coax more memories that might help me learn why I'm here, or who is behind this sick video, but I'm not getting anything useful.

At lunch, I head straight to the cafeteria where Pete and Billy always meet for lunch. They sometimes eat with other kids, but it's usually the two of them since there are three lunch periods and most of Pete's drama friends — the group he hangs out with most — are in the other periods.

When I see him, he races toward me, hardly able to contain his excitement.

"OMG," he says, pulling me away from the lunch line. He drags me out of the cafeteria, finding a spot in the common area out of earshot from anyone.

"What did you find out?"

"I think I know who did it."

"No way. Who?"

"You've got to promise not to do anything crazy."

I shove him in the chest, not hard, but not exactly playful. "Tell me!"

"Well, everyone I talked to said they heard about the video from Rocco. He was practically a one-man advertising campaign."

Anthony Rocco is a cornerback on the school's football team — an obnoxious, entitled asshole made even more obnoxious and entitled because of his parents' wealth. He's also a giant, at least a foot taller than Billy, with at least fifty pounds more muscle on his frame. And even more relevant: Rocco's rumored to have date raped a few girls. Nobody knows if it's only hearsay, or if his father, a high-profile lawyer, managed to pay the girls' families off to keep things at a whisper. Regardless, he's a known sexist pig, and could easily be behind this video.

I start walking back to the cafeteria.

"Billy? Billy? What are you doing?"

I keep walking, my eyes scanning the lunchroom.

I see Rocco toward the back of the room, sitting in a swarm of jocks and cheerleaders, the insincere blonde and redhead who approached me this morning among them.

Rocco is big and tan, with short dark hair and a wide smile. He looks like he failed at least five times, and should be playing college ball.

Even though I'm a good eight tables away, they're

looking up at me, smiles on their smug faces, some of them giggling.

Rage courses through me.

Pete runs up behind me. "Dude, what the hell are you doing?"

I ignore him.

I march forward, eyes locked on Rocco, heart racing and knees shaking. I ignore the fear, fueled by rage.

I make it to the table and am vaguely aware of Pete falling back a bit behind me. History says he'll have my back if this comes to a fight, but he's clearly uncomfortable taking on a fair share of the football team. But before I can consider the logic of what I'm about to do, I'm standing at the table, glaring at the jocks.

Blake Wellington, the six-foot-two blond-haired, blue-eyed quarterback is sitting next to Rocco. Even if he hadn't been blessed with his model good looks or his talent with a ball, he'd still have won the gene lottery by virtue of being born to Dean Wellington, one of Oregon's largest landowners.

Before I can choke out a word to Rocco, Blake eyes me up and down and says, "You lost, Preacher Boy?"

Laughter from the others.

I glare at the blonde and redhead. The blonde meets my gaze, almost challenging me to say something while the redhead stares at the floor.

I ignore Blake and turn to Rocco. "Why did you do that?"

He looks at me, thick eyebrows furrowed in a knot. "Do *what?*"

Everyone's looking at me. I feel like half of them are dying to hear me say something about the video.

"You know what."

"No, I don't," he says, standing up.

"The *video*," I say, practically whispering the word. "Why did you make her do that?"

Rocco looks genuinely surprised. "Make her? You talking about the little porn video your sister made? You think *I* made her do that?"

His emphasis on the word *I* instead of *made* makes me wonder if I'm accusing the wrong person.

"I heard that you made her do it." The words sound so frail on their way out of my mouth that I'm instantly regretting not thinking this through. The fact that a half-wit jock is outsmarting me, assuming that somewhere out there I'm an adult of reasonable intelligence, makes me want to retreat with my tail between my legs.

But I can't let these morons win, and need to find out who did this to Chelsea.

"She told me," I lie before I can think of something more clever.

Rocco leaps over the table so fast I barely have time to back up.

He's on me in seconds, hands around my throat.

"Then the little slut lied!"

"Whoa, whoa, let's all calm down," Pete says, trying to put a hand between Rocco and me.

Rocco lets go of me long enough to shove Pete.

He stumbles back but manages to stay on his feet. Then Pete raises his fists, challenging Rocco.

I don't want him getting his ass kicked because of me, so I stand between them.

Rocco glares at me, his smug smile curling into something ugly, daring me to do something.

I oblige and take a swing.

I'm surprised when he doesn't dodge my fist, and my blow finds his jaw.

Rocco falls back, covering his face in surprise.

Four of the jocks leap to their feet.

Rocco grunts, "I'm gonna kill you!"

Shit is about to get real.

"Whoa, whoa, whoa, gentlemen!" Blake stands, launches himself over the table like Rocco, and steps in front of me, a barrier to Rocco's aggression.

Blake's eyes are intense, but his smile is friendly as he puts his hands on Rocco's chest. "Chill, chill. Kid's sister is in a coma; he's not thinking straight."

He looks back at me as a silent message to stand down, or he'll let Rocco and the others beat our asses.

Suddenly, a tall black man in thick glasses with a shiny bald head is making a beeline toward us. Dean Pritchard.

His voice is deep, his eyes serious. "What's going on here?"

I'm tempted to tell him, but what do I say? Do I tell him about the video? I suddenly realize how much I'm in over my head, being impetuous with another person's life, possibly an entire family's welfare, if this video goes viral beyond the school — assuming it hasn't already.

Blake says, "Everything is fine. Just a bit of a misunderstanding, but it's okay. Billy's been through a lot the past two days."

Dean Pritchard looks me up and down. "That right, Billy?"

A loud voice inside me is screaming, *Say something!*, but I can't. I need to slow down and *think* about my next move. Do I tell an adult about the video? Or Billy's parents? What if Chelsea comes out of her coma to disappointed parents who shame her further?

"Are you okay, Billy?" Pritchard asks after I say nothing.

I swallow and finally meet his eyes, nodding. "Yeah, just a misunderstanding."

Dean Pritchard looks at me, then at Blake. I'm wondering if he's buying Wellington's bullshit. He looks like he's thinking about it. Maybe thinking about dragging us all to his office where we can get to the bottom of whatever this is. But then his lips tighten, and he says, "Okay, well why don't you all separate."

Surprised, I nod.

Pete and I turn, leaving the scene of my embarrassment. I can feel Rocco and his friends' gazes on our backs.

Once we make it back to the common area, Pete leads us down a few hallways until we find one that's quiet.

He leans against the wall and sinks to the ground. "Oh my God, what happened to promising not to do anything stupid?"

"You said not to do anything *crazy*," I remind him with a grin, "you never said not to do anything *stupid*."

"Sorry, I assumed suicidal was on the list under crazy."

His eyes widen as he realizes he just used what I imagine will now forever be called "the s-word" in Billy's company if Chelsea doesn't pull through. "I'm sorry. I didn't mean to …"

"It's okay."

"But seriously, what the hell was that?"

"I dunno. I just wanted to know who was responsible."

"Have you *ever* watched a detective story? The detective never goes straight at the suspect, not without some evidence, or *something!* Man, the art of subtlety is lost on you, Billy Boy."

"I had something … your word. If you say Rocco is the one who did it, I trust you."

"Well, shit, I didn't say I knew for certain! I think it's him, yeah, but I don't *know*."

"So, what was I supposed to do?"

"I figured we'd tell someone, maybe the police or

18

something. Let them investigate. But now you probably screwed that all up. If it *is* him, he's probably gonna go home and delete anything on his computer, phone, whatever he used, and we won't have dick."

"Shit!"

I look down, staring at the tile floor.

Suddenly, I hear movement.

I look up to see the redhead cheerleader cautiously approaching.

Pete sits up straight, defensive. "What do *you* want, Becca?"

"I'm sorry about your sister," she says, meeting my eyes. For all her friend's insincerity, I get the opposite from Becca. She seems genuinely concerned.

"Yeah, me too," I say, my eyes up from the floor and now staring at the wall, not wanting to look at her for reasons I'm not sure of. Maybe I still don't trust her. And nothing would pain me more than to offer one of Chelsea's enemies Billy's naive trust.

"Listen," she says, "I don't know what you think Rocco did — if he actually recorded the video, or what. But I don't think it was him."

I stand and finally meet her eyes. Pete rises beside me and says, "What do you mean? He's been passing it around like Skittles."

"Yeah, Rocco and a lot of other guys have been. But that doesn't mean they recorded the video."

"So," I say, "who do you think did it?"

"Someone she was sleeping with."

"My sister wasn't sleeping with anyone. She didn't have a boyfriend."

"No, not exactly."

"What are you saying?" I ask, my voice growing louder.

"There are rumors that Chelsea was sleeping with one of the teachers."

"What?"

Pete echoes my thought. "I haven't heard that, and I hear everything!"

"I don't know how many people know. Fewer than the number who know about the video, but I think it's something you should probably look into."

"Who?" I ask.

"Ms. Valencia, her art teacher."

"No way," I say. "Chelsea's not gay. And she certainly isn't sleeping with a teacher!"

Becca looks down. "I don't know what to tell you so that you'll believe me. I just thought you'd like to know, and so maybe you don't go getting yourself killed by Rocco."

"What do you care?" I ask. "*They're* your friends, not *me*."

"Yeah," she says, looking at her crossed feet, "but that doesn't mean I want to see you get hurt, or that I like some of the stuff they do. I liked Chelsea. We haven't been friends for a couple of years, but that doesn't mean I hate her or think she's a *dyke*, or a slut, or deserves this bullshit."

"If you like my sister, then why are you friends with these assholes who think it's funny to slut shame her, to spread her video around until she tries to kill herself?"

Becca looks back up. "I wish I had a good answer. Sorry."

And with that, she turns around and walks away.

I look at Pete, who, for once, is speechless.

∽

BILLY'S DAD picks me up, on the phone — *again*. Still talking to his agent. I wonder if he is always this disconnected from his kids, or if this is an anomaly due to the family's world crumbling around them.

It's just as well. I still haven't decided how to tell him about the video, or if I even should.

He drops me off at home and says he's going to the hospital with Mom. This gives me time to search Chelsea's room, see if I can find anything to verify that she was sleeping with Ms. Valencia.

As I cross the threshold into her room — a tidy room with eggshell-white walls, pastel accents, and soft-edged white furniture with clean angles and uncluttered surfaces — I think about all the bedrooms I've been an interloper in. After a while, one blends right into another. But all bedrooms are a place to keep treasures, particularly secrets of the heart — private loves, old flames, obsessions — tucked in the pages of journals, love letters buried in the closet, way in the back, or mementos buried in plain sight. Enter someone's bedroom, and you'll find what resides in their heart.

If Chelsea *was* sleeping with her teacher, I'm guessing I'll find the evidence here.

I start in the usual places, desk, closet, under the mattress and bed, but find nothing incriminating.

There's nothing in her computer, either, at least not that jumps out with a cursory search.

Since Chelsea, like Billy, is a neat freak, it doesn't take long to go through her stuff, yet after thirty minutes, I've found nothing.

I sit on her bed, frustrated, looking around the room for any spot I might have missed or didn't think to look.

Lying on her bed, I feel a lump beneath the blanket.

I reach down and find Pinky, a stuffed pink unicorn she got as a child and has slept with ever since.

I look at the unicorn, tears welling in my eyes as memories of Chelsea and Billy's lives flash by. Billy, being four years younger, always looked up to his sister. As children, they'd been inseparable; Chelsea loved having a baby brother and, once he could walk, brought him with her wherever she went. When Billy was four, his sister bought him a "boy's version" of the unicorn, a blue one, which he named Bluey, even if it wasn't a *real name*. They often had "campouts" indoors, setting up makeshift tents made of sheets and blankets in the living room, where they'd play with their unicorns.

Suddenly, another memory.

During one of their campouts, Pinky told Billy about a loose floorboard in her hallway between their bedrooms where she could pass super-secret spy messages to Bluey. They used the spot for a couple of years passing "secrets" to each other. Then, around the time that Chelsea went to seventh grade, the messages stopped. Suddenly, she was too busy to play Unicorn Spies with her brother.

I get up from her bed, then go to the hallway and search for the loose board.

My heart races as my fingers find the wooden plank.

I pull it up at the edge.

Inside the small dark space, I see a blue hardbound book: Chelsea's diary.

I'M SITTING at the kitchen table waiting for Billy's parents to come home. The diary is sitting closed before me.

I've learned two things from the journal.

One — Chelsea *was* sleeping with Ms. Valencia. Not

just sleeping with her, but *in love* with her. Had been since the beginning of the school year, though she didn't start sleeping with her until two months ago, well after she turned eighteen, something Ms. Valencia insisted upon, even though Chelsea wanted to be with her earlier.

Two — she was coerced into stripping on camera. A few weeks ago, someone, she doesn't know who, messaged Chelsea with photos of her and the teacher taken from just outside a hotel room window. They said if she didn't "perform" for them, they'd leak the photos to "every news site known to man."

Scared, Chelsea did as she was told.

The last page in her diary she wrote to Billy:

~

BILLY,

I knew you'd find this. Please don't show Mom and Dad. They'll be furious. They'll try and get Ms. Valencia fired, or worse. You know how Dad gets.

But I want YOU to know the truth.

YOU deserve to know why I had to do it.

Yes, the rumors are true. I am gay. I know you won't care because you're not like Mom and Dad. And your best friend is Pete, who is the gayest gay dude ever.

Ms. Valencia was the first person to make me feel like I wasn't a freak. The first person who made me feel okay with who I am.

I tried to keep it a secret, at least until I was out of school, off at college, away from the family.

But then THIS happened.

That awful video. I'm so ashamed. And now the name calling in the halls — slut, dyke, bitch. And they weren't even the worst part. It was the whispers, the judgmental looks. The wondering if the person

*I'm talking to, hell, the teacher I'm talking to, didn't see that video —
hadn't seen me at my most vulnerable, most ashamed.*

I just couldn't take it.

*I know you always looked up to me and thought I was so strong,
and brave. And I hate that you now see the truth.*

I'm not strong.

I'm not brave.

And I can't pretend any longer.

*I'm sorry to leave you like this. And I want you to know that
none of this is your fault. There's nothing you could've done
differently.*

I know you love me unconditionally.

But I just couldn't take the shit any longer.

I hope now that I'm gone, the fuckers will leave you in peace.

I love you.

~

LOVE,
  Chelsea

~

P.S. PLEASE TAKE care of Pinky.

~

I CRIED the entire time I read it. I'm sickened to think that
anyone would end their life because of bullying, and this
makes me want to hurt Rocco and the others even more
than I already did.

Chelsea didn't want her parents to see this, but I have
to overrule her. They *need* to see it. They need to know why

their daughter tried to kill herself, and understand their culpability.

I hear the front door open, the sound of Jack's keys being dropped in the bowl.

Billy's parents enter the kitchen, surprised to see me sitting there.

"What's that?" Jack asks.

I tell them. Everything.

Chapter Two

I WAKE up to the ringing of my phone on the nightstand.

Not *my* phone, Jack Caldwell's.

I grab the phone, see that it's only six in the morning, and am hoping it's not the hospital calling to tell me that Chelsea is dead.

It's not Chelsea; it's Waylon, Jack's agent.

"You up?" Waylon says in a slight Southern drawl. He grew up in Louisiana, played some college ball, then got hurt and entered law school, specializing in entertainment. From there, he became an agent, landing some of the biggest names in reality TV. Jack was his first Christian author, but he's proved himself in steering his client away from ministry-type work and toward life as a self-help guru, increasing Jack's net worth tenfold in the first year alone.

"Yeah, hold on," I say, climbing out of bed, leaving Susan sleeping as I make my way out of the bedroom, downstairs, and into Jack's study. I wait for his tired mind to fill me in on what happened — from Jack's perspective — after Billy dropped the bomb last night.

From Billy's perspective, it was a scary moment. At

first, his parents stared. Then came the tears — followed by anger.

Jack was so pissed that he stormed out of the house, going God knew where for several hours. Jack's memories tell me he went to a bar and got drunk — something he hasn't done in nearly fifteen years.

When I, as Billy, had asked why Dad was so mad, Susan said, "Because that teacher ruined our Chelsea. She made her gay."

I had argued otherwise, saying, "You can't *make* someone gay. They either are or aren't."

That didn't sit well with Susan.

"That's just something the Devil and his followers say, to convince you that sin is okay. 'Hey, it's not my fault, I was born this way.' Sorry, Billy, that's not how it works. I know you have a homosexual friend, and while your father doesn't care for it, I like Pete. But that doesn't mean I condone his behavior ... or Chelsea's."

I wanted to argue more, but in my experience, you can't change someone overnight, and I didn't want to get Billy into trouble with his family. They had enough going on already, without a volatile religious argument added to the mix.

I enter Jack's office, close the door, and sit at his desk.

"All right, shoot," I say, remembering how Jack was talking in the car yesterday. I'm not sure exactly what Waylon called to say, but I figure it must be something worthwhile if he's doing it this early.

"Well, I looked into this teacher a bit. And as long as Chelsea consented to sex after she was eighteen there's nothing we can do, legally."

"Really?" I say, surprised.

"Yeah, some politician in California tried to get a bill made into law to prohibit teacher-student relationships, arguing that a teacher could groom a student before they're of age, but it went nowhere, and that's further than it's gone here."

"Wow," I say, not knowing what to add. I'm not sure what Jack would say in this situation, and don't want to light any unintended fireworks.

Waylon clears his throat. "While we can't do anything legally, we can make this bitch's life a nightmare. She's going to lose her job the minute this is reported, might never be able to teach again, maybe lose her benefits. But we can go further. I say we call the police and tell them you suspect the relationship may have started sooner."

"But Chelsea's diary said it wasn't until she was eighteen."

"Yeah, but it's at least possible that she lied, right? Maybe to protect this teacher she's in love with. Who's to say that this woman didn't see Chelsea a year ago and start grooming her then, maybe convinced her to take an art class? We don't *know* the truth, right, so it could be anything is all I'm saying."

"I suppose."

"Good. Now for this video nastiness, I've got my guy on it — an ex-detective, half bulldog named Mike Arrinson. He's gonna chase down some of these porn sites and say the video with Chelsea is blackmail porn, which is illegal in some states. Then he can add that it's *possible* that Chelsea was underage when she did that video, which should scare most of the legit sites from serving it."

"Legit sites?"

"Well, yeah, you can't get it down from everywhere. There are always some pervs who will be sharing it on less-than-reputable sites. Maybe they'll even upload it to image boards, who knows? I'm sorry to say there's no way to get the genie back in the bottle. Chelsea's video is out there.

Assuming she comes out of this coma, this is going to haunt her forever."

I sigh. I want to make the person who did this pay.

"Can we find out who blackmailed her?"

"I can have Mike dig around. It's gonna be tough because if we're dealing with minors, we're limited in what we can do, legally."

The way he keeps saying *legally* makes me wonder if he's opening the door for Jack to suggest less-than-legal methods.

I don't bite.

"And these kids at your school have rich, connected parents, making shit that much more difficult. Fortunately, I have a few connections at the police department, and I might be able to figure something out."

"Thanks," I say.

"Now, one last thing, Jack. And this isn't me as your agent, so much as me as your friend. Are you sure you want to go forward with this story?"

"You mean go to the police?"

"Yeah."

"Why wouldn't we?"

"Well, for one, we've got the suicide note that you didn't mention to them. Right now, this is a case of accidental overdose, not a suicide attempt. Different story in the public eye."

Jack's memories tell me that keeping the note secret was at Waylon's *strongly advised* suggestion. "You're the one who told me not to give them the note."

"And I stand by that decision. We can easily say that the note was in the diary. You'll just need to get your family on board if that's the story we're going with. But we've also got to consider the elephant in the room."

"What elephant?"

"That TV series you're starting next month. This is Big Time, Jack. The network gets a hint of your daughter being a lesbian, or this sex tape, or the affair with the teacher, you can kiss this deal goodbye."

I didn't know Jack had signed a TV deal, meaning I don't think he told his children yet. Jack's memories confirm as much. He wanted to surprise the kids, take them to the pilot episode's taping. The show had been a dream of his forever, and Waylon had helped Jack to make it reality — a daily syndicated self-help show that could make him a household name, not just among his fellow Christians, but among the mainstream — where the big money and endorsements are. This deal could be life-changing not just for Jack and his family, but for the world, the way Jack saw it. He could spread the Gospel in a less preachy way, through actions instead of only words. It had been his dream for years to give hope to the hopeless, and now he was poised to do exactly that. Waylon was right: If word got out about any of this, it would instantly crush his reputation. The TV deal would evaporate.

His image forever tainted.

And just like that, an empire on the verge of creation crumbles to dust.

What kind of Christian self-help guru could he possibly be if he couldn't even see the darkness under his roof? A lesbian daughter sleeping with her teacher — who then tries to kill herself — isn't the way to inspire confidence in the Jack Caldwell brand.

And these days, everything is about the brand.

After thinking about it for a moment, I say, "But won't this get out anyway? Half of her school is already talking about the video. At least a few people know about her teacher. I don't see how we can possibly keep this quiet."

"Maybe not forever, but we can bottle it long enough to

capitalize on the pilot. Get some stories out there about how you're gonna change the face of daytime television, how you'll be a bright light in a deluge of despair. Shit would probably blow up before pilot season, and the show would never air, but then we've got a *new* story, maybe a pitch for another show — where you acknowledge your weaknesses, and how God has brought you and your family closer than ever in the aftermath of this tragedy."

I'm not sure if I should marvel at Waylon's ability to spin disaster or be sickened by it.

"And what if Chelsea dies? Or what if she comes out of the coma, but hates me for disapproving of her lifestyle? What then?"

"Well, it might be a tough sell to the evangelicals, but we'll find a way to make it work — whatever it is. Maybe we can have her deprogrammed. Or maybe you convert to a less-restrictive version of your faith. Christianity is big numbers and bigger money, but there are more and more disenfranchised every day, Jack. We could make a home for all those who feel abandoned by their faith. Hell, I can almost see a ministry being born out of this! Does your Jesus hate gays? Well, leave that old-school Jesus behind, and come to an all-loving God who will accept you just the way you are. Hell, why stop at gays? We can attract all the freaks who are tired of being judged. Into bestiality, kids? We've got ya covered here at Jack Caldwell's Heavenly Outreach."

Waylon breaks down laughing.

I'm not sure what to think of this man. He obviously has giant balls to insult Jack's daughter's sexuality and insinuate that his faith is merely for show. I wonder if he has precedent for this. Has Jack given Waylon a reason to doubt his faith, to make his agent think he's nothing more than a charlatan out for money?

I feel that Jack's faith is real, but it's hard to tell from the memories he's provided so far. I ignore Waylon's comments, and say, "Please, just do what you can to find out who did this to Chelsea."

"So, you wanna go to the police?"

"Yes," I say.

"Okay, don't call anyone yet. I'll get started on a press release. Then I'll head on over to your place so we can walk through this together. After that, you make the call."

I'm annoyed that I have to wait to call the police, but at the same time, Jack's in the limelight, and it would be easy for me to screw this all up. I accept Waylon's offer and hang up.

I'm sitting in the police station, waiting for Detective Kevin Wilson's return. His partner, Lucy Jimenez, has just coached me through what I'll need to say during a controlled phone call to Ms. Valencia, designed to get Chelsea's teacher to admit her crime on record.

I'm feeling uneasy about this, especially if the teacher hasn't committed a crime. Chelsea's journal says she was eighteen when this all started. While I'm sickened that a teacher would sleep with any student, seeing as it is a complete betrayal of custodianship, I don't want to trick her into a confession that could land her behind bars if it isn't against the law.

The detectives spent most of the morning questioning our family, going over details of the journal, and the suicide note we claimed to have found just this morning. Additionally, they took Chelsea's laptop and phone to see if they could find any evidence against the teacher and any clues as to who was blackmailing her.

I sent Susan and Billy back to the house. Waylon is at the station with me; I suppose to make sure I don't say anything stupid.

After a while, Detective Wilson comes in. He escorts me and Waylon to another room with one phone hooked up to another, and a recording device. I sit in one of the two chairs, Waylon taking a spot beside me.

Detective Jimenez is also there, standing in front of the table. "You remember everything we went over? Start off slow, and don't use any words like rape or abuse, or mention legality. We don't want to scare her off. You're calling as Chelsea's parent, concerned over what your daughter told you before she passed out."

"Okay," I say nodding.

Detective Wilson hands me a piece of paper with Ms. Valencia's number.

I dial, my heart racing.

After a few rings, she answers.

"Hello?"

"Ms. Valencia?"

"Yes, who's calling?"

"This is Jack Caldwell, Chelsea's father."

A moment of silence, followed by, "Oh, hello, Mr. Caldwell. I'm so sorry to hear about Chelsea. How is she doing?"

"She's still in the hospital, still in a coma."

I was instructed not to lie and say there was a good chance she might come out of the coma, as we don't know if that would make the teacher more or less likely to say something.

"I'm sorry," Ms. Valencia says. Her voice sounds pleasant, caring, a slight Spanish accent. "How can I help you?"

I look up at Detective Jimenez, listening on the other phone. She nods, giving me the courage to work the script.

"I just wanted to call because I know how close you were to my daughter, to let you know that she left some art at the house she wanted me to give you. She left it in her note."

Another moment of silence. I can tell that Ms. Valencia is likely wondering if I know *how close* she was to Chelsea.

"Her note?"

"Yes, we haven't made it public, but Chelsea tried to kill herself."

"Oh, God. I was afraid of this."

Detective Jimenez meets my eyes and nods, indicating that I'm doing well.

"You know she was having problems?"

"Well, yeah, she told me that some kids were bothering her."

"How so?" I ask.

Another pause. "Well, you know how kids are. They say mean things to one another. Sometimes, they can get pretty ugly, single someone out, and make their life difficult."

I wonder if I should ask why she didn't call me to let me know that Chelsea was having issues, but the detectives urged me to keep things friendly as long as possible. The minute I put her on the defense, it will become difficult to get her back to that comfortable level. They also coached me on tactics to use if things do get ugly, to insinuate that I know something I don't, to accuse her, to see if she verifies it in any way. *Get a verification, you get a hell of a better case.*

"What sorts of things did they say?"

She pauses again, maybe senses where this is going. I need to be careful.

"Well, the usual things. They made fun of her for being

a 'pastor's daughter' ... they called her a prude, and ... some of them started rumors, saying she was a ... slut."

The last word comes out bluntly, like she isn't sure how to say it. I wonder if she's afraid where that word will take this conversation, or merely doesn't want to say something so awful about Jack's daughter.

"What kind of rumors?"

A longer pause. "I don't know the specifics, just hurtful things that kids tend to say about one another."

"Well, I want to thank you for being there for her. I know it can't be easy for her to be my daughter, what with her homosexuality and all. It's good that she had you to help her come to terms."

A very long pause now. I sense she might be about to go on the defensive. I decide to go all-in.

"Listen, I know you were having an affair with my daughter. She told me everything. And while I wasn't pleased, at first, she's eighteen and can do whatever she wants. Truth is, her being in a coma has put this all in perspective for me. I just want her to get better. I want my little girl back."

Silence, at first, followed by her tears.

"I'm not mad," I say. "I was surprised, as I suppose any father might be. But love is love — we don't control who we fall in love with. Right?"

"No, we do not. I just want to say that I never intended to fall in love with your daughter, Mr. Caldwell. I know how awful this must appear. And nothing ever happened between us until *after* she'd turned eighteen."

"I know I've been hard on my daughter, have been a bit — okay, a lot — overprotective, but that's only because I love Chelsea and want her to be happy. If that happiness happens to be with you, so be it."

"Wow," Ms. Valencia says. "I don't know what to say."

"There's no need to say anything. As far as I'm concerned, you're family."

"Wow. Um, thank you, Mr. Caldwell."

I look up at Detective Jimenez, who's giving me a thumbs-up.

I got a confession of a relationship, which was the heavy lifting. Now, if I can get her to admit she slept with Chelsea before she was eighteen, the detectives will have what they need.

I tread slowly, "Um, there's just one thing that doesn't make sense."

"What's that?" Ms. Valencia asks, her voice betraying frazzled nerves. She can sense the hook. I need to be careful, or I'll lose her.

"Well, you said you all didn't get together until she was eighteen, but Chelsea told me something different, and she wrote something else in her diary — saying it began four months ago, which would be a month *before* she turned eighteen."

A long pause.

I'm not sure if this means she's busted, and she *was*, in fact, sleeping with Chelsea before she turned eighteen, or if she's surprised that Chelsea would lie. Maybe she's doing the math in her head? Or, a third option, she knows this call is being recorded.

What do I do if she asks if she's being recorded? I can't remember if the detectives covered that scenario or not.

They must have, right?

But I can't remember.

Shit.

The longer her silence stretches, the more certain I am that she's busted *me*.

Nothing.

Come on, talk!

Finally, she speaks. "I don't know why she'd say that. Chelsea *was* eighteen. We specifically waited. She *wanted* to be with me on the night of her eighteenth birthday, you know, to celebrate, but she said you were bringing her to dinner at her favorite restaurant, Christopher's Steak House. It was a school night — a Tuesday if I recall — so we waited until the following weekend."

Now I'm the one who is quiet.

She was so specific, and her details match Chelsea's diary. They waited. I don't think she's lying, and I don't want to push her or trick her into a false confession. This is her life on the line and could be the difference between her *just* being fired and going to jail, registering as a sex offender, or whatever other punishment she'd face for sleeping with a minor.

I don't look at Detective Jimenez. I say, "Maybe I'm mistaken. Sorry. Listen, I've gotta go. I'll call you some other time to arrange picking up the stuff Chelsea wanted you to have."

A beat of silence. Then, "Um, okay. Thank you for calling."

"Thank you," I say, hanging up.

Chapter Three

I WAKE up in a room so dark and cold it feels like a tomb. Given my hangover, maybe it's fitting.

It takes a moment for the cobwebs to clear, but I soon realize I'm inside Carla Valencia, Chelsea's art teacher.

I sit up, head pounding as fragments of last night's memories rush through my head: Carla getting the phone call from Jack Caldwell, trying to keep her cool, then breaking down in tears the moment she hung up. The feeling of absolute loneliness as she lay on the floor crying, knowing that her career was over; and the walls were closing in.

And then the walls did close in — two detectives at her front door, asking her to come to the station and answer some questions. Before they left, they presented a warrant to search her premises. They didn't take her away in cuffs, but may as well have. She felt a deep shame as her next-door neighbor, Mrs. Abrams, watched the detectives escorting Carla to their cruiser from her porch.

This was everything she'd feared from the moment her

relationship with Chelsea crossed the line from friendship to more.

She'd waited until the girl was eighteen, but that wouldn't spare her from losing everything — her career, her reputation, the possibility of ever teaching children again. No one would trust her. They'd all think she was some kind of pervert, deviant, a monster.

The police let her go after five long, excruciating hours of questioning, attempts to trip her up, to get to some "truth" they felt she was hiding. They were at turns nice, understanding, and accusing. Carla felt like she was being interviewed by schizophrenics, and by the end of the five hours, barely knew which way was up. She was reasonably certain that if they kept her any longer, she might slip. Not that she'd let out some incriminating truth — because she *hadn't* slept with the girl before she was eighteen — but in her confusion, she might make a mistake, say something that wasn't true, or which they could use against her. She was close to asking for a lawyer a few times but was afraid she'd look guilty the minute she did. Carla thought the cops believed her, but you could never tell, especially when they were all over the place throughout the questioning. She couldn't tell what they were saying to persuade her, or play on her emotions, versus what was real.

No matter what the police believed, this would still go public. And nobody would ever see Carla the same. All the good she'd done as a teacher, all the students she'd helped by going the extra mile, showing them the beauty of art. She'd done a lot of good. She'd changed lives. Some of her students would go on to great careers because Carla had lit that fire inside them.

But that would all be meaningless once this story was public.

And while Carla could see why people wouldn't understand why she'd throw her career away for a "child," as the detectives described Chelsea, those people didn't know the girl or understand their connection.

She went to bed afraid — afraid for her career, afraid for her life, afraid the police might return with charges to arrest her. But even more than all of that, she was afraid for Chelsea, that she might not make it out of this.

After she got home, Carla had to call her mother and tell her everything — not an easy conversation. Her mother had been surprisingly supportive. She cried, said she didn't understand how a woman in her thirties could fall for a child. The conversation had many parallels to when Carla came out to her, also by phone, in her first semester of college, at the urging of Carla's first love, Laura. Mom was resistant, at first, but eventually supported her daughter's decision. And while she didn't advocate Carla sleeping with a student, she did offer to pay for her legal support, should it be needed.

I finish showering and get dressed, choosing sweat pants and a long T-shirt, as I have no intentions of leaving the house as Carla. I have no idea who knows what and don't want to do anything that might screw things up, either for her or the investigation.

Her apartment is small but nice.

I go into the second bedroom, which has been turned into an art studio. Framed on the wall is an almost photo-realistic colored pencil sketch of an eye. Not just any eye; it's Carla's eye, drawn by Chelsea.

This was sketched early in their relationship, during the phase where they both knew there was something happening between them, but neither would move. Chelsea was too scared. Carla was still in denial, trying not to act on her feelings.

Carla thought she'd never love again, not after cancer had taken Laura five years ago.

She certainly didn't think she'd fall for a student. But Chelsea was the first person since Laura whom Carla felt such an instant connection with.

As a kid, Carla had never been one to believe in soul mates. It seemed like the stuff that romance novels, movies, and greeting cards were built around, but which didn't exist for everyday people. Of course, at the time, Carla was still in denial thinking she simply needed to meet the right boy. Who knew the right boy wouldn't be a boy at all, but rather a girl she'd meet as a college freshman, a girl who would change her every notion about love and fate.

Laura had been the one. An artist and poet. She even played guitar. She saw things nobody else saw and said them in ways that no one else could. It was as if Fate had sought what Carla's soul had been craving and decided to make a person for her alone.

Carla could truly be herself with Laura. She helped Carla to realize her potential, made her want to be something, to inspire others. Laura had been so full of life until Fate snuffed her out across six cruel months.

Forget love, Carla never thought she'd smile or laugh again. Only through teaching did she find any joy, and for a long time, that was enough. She would live in honor of Laura, inspiring others.

Then Carla met Chelsea, the last person in the world she'd expect to be so perfect for her. Chelsea was the daughter of a religious self-help guru and conservative mother, an uptight girl afraid of life. But over time, she slowly left her shell in such a way that Carla couldn't help but take notice. She started coming to class after school, at first under the pretense of extra tutelage. Soon, instruction gave way to long conversations. Chelsea wanted to know about Carla's life, the things she enjoyed in her off time, and what she thought about big subjects.

And as ridiculous as it seemed at first, Carla found herself wanting to know the same about the girl.

She'd tried to talk herself out of her developing feelings. Asked herself a question her mother would later ask: What could a high school student know about anything to make her interesting? What life experience could she possibly have? And for a while, that argument worked. Chelsea wasn't like Laura, full of all these crazy experiences, bold and daring, unafraid and unapologetic in her approach to life. No, Chelsea was more like Carla as she'd been when she'd met her first love. And Carla was now the one with experiences, who was (somewhat) bold and unapologetic. It was almost as if Carla had somehow gone back in time and reversed roles, except now *she* was the one helping another girl to discover herself, and, eventually, her sexuality.

But it wasn't all the reanimation of a relationship gone by. Carla was genuinely intrigued by Chelsea. She had original ideas about art, in all its forms. For a girl living with such repressive parents, Chelsea had one of the most creative minds Carla had ever seen — but hidden beneath layers of fear and insecurity.

Chelsea was a beautiful, rare flower waiting for someone to tell her just how beautiful and rare she was.

And even though she tried to fight the feeling, Carla wanted to be that person.

She couldn't stop thinking about Chelsea, wondering what she was doing, wondering what sort of conversation they'd have next, what new layer of the onion the girl might reveal. She was a mystery, a lovely *forbidden* mystery.

After feeling Chelsea's love, Carla wasn't sure she could live without it.

I look around the studio and notice a half-finished painting in the corner, sitting on an easel. It shows a woman's shoulder and the nape of her neck, brown locks of hair cascading down her back. A nude of Carla draped beneath a white robe, which Chelsea had been in the process of painting. Chelsea was more skilled with a brush than she was with a pencil, but you could see her raw talent just looking at the composition, brush strokes, and palette. Art wasn't just what you decided to focus on, but often just as much about what was left out. And in this instance, the framing of Carla's body and the placement of her robe were different from how most artists would've painted her.

I reach out to touch the painting, and a crushing realization hits me: *Chelsea may never finish the portrait.*

Tears sting my eyes.

Being inside Carla is too intense. Her feelings too raw. It's hard to separate myself from her, harder still to feel the anger I felt before when I was in Billy and Jack. Then, I was angry at this woman for stealing *my sister*, stealing *my daughter*, for taking advantage of a child.

But being inside Carla, I don't get the sense that she was some dangerous predator looking to take advantage of naive students. She wasn't looking for sex. She wasn't even looking for love. She fought it. No, not hard enough, but I find it difficult to blame her as much as I did before.

Yes, she was wrong to sleep with a student. She likely destroyed her life and may have contributed to Chelsea's death, but I no longer feel like she exploited or took advantage of Chelsea. In many ways, you could make the argument that she helped her become a strong young woman, no longer hiding from her true self — embracing her sexuality instead of denying it as a Devil's temptation.

If only you hadn't slept with her.

And there is Carla's fatal flaw — a weakness, a loneliness she wasn't strong enough to overcome.

I'm not sure how I would feel if this were to happen to my child. I doubt I could ever understand it. Doubt I could ever forgive. If Carla hadn't slept with Chelsea, hadn't been so careless as to be seen by someone who had somehow managed to record video of the two of them in Carla's bed, then Chelsea would never have been black-mailed or bullied. She would never have tried to kill herself.

None of this would've happened if Carla had kept her distance, *at least* waited for the girl to graduate.

Being inside Carla, I feel pity and compassion for what her life is about to become. If Chelsea dies, the guilt will kill her.

As I stare at the paintings, I can't take any more.

I need to get out of Carla's place, take a drive, do something to take my mind away from all of this shit.

I change my clothes, putting on a blue skirt and matching top. I slip on some flats, grab Carla's purse, phone, and car keys, then head out the door.

In the hallway outside of Carla's apartment, a skinny white man in a baseball cap is approaching me.

At first, I don't recognize him.

By the time I do, it's too late.

He's suddenly on me, shoving a rag against my face.

MY HEAD IS POUNDING, my vision blurry as I wake up to the sound of footsteps echoing off walls in what sounds like a large empty space. I'm sitting in a chair, hands tied behind my back, a gag in my mouth preventing any cries for help.

I open my eyes to a blinding light, and can't see anything of my captor, save for a shadow behind the light.

"Well, well, well, look who decided to wake up and join the party," says a voice I'm all too familiar with.

I squirm, trying to loosen the binds.

"Hey, hey, did I say you can move?" Jack Caldwell approaches me with something in his hand.

I don't see what it is, but feel the jolts as they enter my body.

Chapter Four

I wake in a chair, startled.

I'm in Susan Caldwell's body. Beside me, in the hospital bed hooked up to machines and life support, is Chelsea.

I'm stunned to see her there sleeping.

I'm seeing her not only as having been in her body, in what feels like ages ago now, but also from the perspective of her father, her brother, her lover, and now her mother. A current of helplessness ripples through me. I'm so close, yet unable to help her, or nudge, her out of unconsciousness.

Wake up, Chelsea. The world needs you.

I reach out to touch her hand, and tears well up in my eyes. I think of all the hell she'd been through, all because of some invisible, anonymous coward.

Poor girl.

And then, after too long of a moment, I remember what happened: I was in Carla's body — Jack had gone nuts and kidnapped her.

I look at the phone.

It's still Saturday. I jumped into Susan's body the second time Carla passed out.

Thankful that Susan nodded off at her daughter's bedside, I need to make good use of the timing. I find the phone in her purse and dial Jack's number hoping like hell he'll pick up and I can talk him out of doing anything stupid. Well, *stupider*.

No answer.

Shit.

Come on, Susan, give me some memory that'll tell me where Jack took her.

After a year, I still can't figure out how to tap into a host brain to get exactly what I need when I need it. I suppose it's miraculous that I get anything, let alone enough info to pass off as the person I'm pretending to be on any given day. But at times like this, I would love some sort of indexed database where I could plug in a few keywords or a question like *places Jack might take a kidnap victim*, and get a response.

I'm getting a vague memory about a cabin in the woods, but nothing that provides a location. I suppose I can go home and search the house to see if we have a deed for a cabin in the woods, but that would take forever, assuming they even had anything readily accessible.

Think, Ella, think.

Waylon! Maybe he even knows what Jack is up to, though I doubt something like this would've earned his sanction.

No, Waylon would not approve.

Jack must've lost his mind. I wonder how much he remembers from when I was in his body — the police station, the phone call, the conversation with Waylon. From what I can tell, people usually retain most of their memories. It's almost as if the brain removes me from the equation. It calls up the history and presents it all to the host as if it happened while they were still on duty. There might be some disassociation, but not enough to where anyone knows they were gone from their body. The brain has a marvelous ability to trick the self.

I have to imagine that when Jack woke up, he remembered what happened, maybe called the police only to learn that they let Carla go, pending investigation. And then he lost it.

Susan's memories confirm my suspicion. She overheard part of a heated call with Waylon this morning, after which Jack hung up and said, "I can't believe they let her go!"

He didn't stick around to explain things. He said he was going for a run, as he often did when agitated — far better than turning to the bottle as he'd done for so many years.

I call Waylon.

"Hello?"

"Are you with Jack?" I ask, voice filled with an urgency he can't help but notice.

"No, why?"

"I think he's done something awful."

"What?"

"I think he'd kidnapped Chelsea's teacher, Ms. Valencia."

"What? What do you mean you think he did? Did he say something?"

"I can't explain how I know. Can you think of anywhere he would've taken her? Somewhere maybe without too much furniture?"

He's quiet for a second, then says, "We have that fishing lodge in the mountains. It's still not furnished."

"That's gotta be it."

"Wait … how do you know he took her? Or that he's got her in some place without furniture?"

Stuck for an answer, I give one that he'll either laugh at or believe. "God told me."

He's quiet.

"I'm at the hospital. Can you take me to the cabin? Like now?"

"On the way, but you better tell me more about this God-told-you stuff."

"Thanks," I say.

AFTER I FILL Waylon in on the lie that God gave me a vision of Jack holding Ms. Valencia hostage, we ride in relative silence. I'm guessing he doesn't believe me, as Waylon seems a bit too street smart for *God told me*. But beyond a raised eyebrow or two, he keeps his skepticism to himself. He likely figures it's something he's better off not knowing, which is good because there's no way I'm telling him the truth: *Hey, I'm not Susan, but rather a woman named Ella who just might be a body-jumping assassin.*

After a while, I say, "Do you think you can convince him to let the teacher go?"

"Don't you worry, Mrs. Caldwell, I'll talk some sense into your husband."

Susan's memories gush forth, giving me some background on her relationship with Jack, a story he wrote in his first book, *Lost, Now Found.*

Jack wasn't a believer when they met in college. He wasn't an atheist, just didn't give much thought to God. Susan was the one who went to church every Sunday, and whose belief was a source of strength. While Susan never thought she'd date, let alone marry, someone who didn't share her faith, Jack was nice and extremely charming. He was also strong and self-confident, but lacking the excessive bravado that was a shared trait among most of the men she knew.

He began his career as a marketer, making a lot of money selling everything from supplements to seminars. It was easy money. *Too* easy. Jack bought into a lifestyle he couldn't maintain — expensive cars, fine clothes, a house beyond their means. And, for a while, everything was fine.

But then his darkness appeared. Jack had a hole inside he was trying to fill, and when money didn't work, he drank, gambled, and cheated.

Susan didn't know what to do. Family and friends urged her to leave him, saying things like: *He's no good. He doesn't deserve a woman like you. You can do so much better.*

But there's one thing they didn't know. Not even Jack knew.

Susan was pregnant with Chelsea.

Even when things were terrible, she couldn't give up on the man she loved, at least not without a fight.

One night she followed him to a bar, then parked her car and waited for him to stumble out of the bar, drunk with some floozy.

Susan got out of her car and stormed up to Jack.

His eyes were wide as she grabbed him, told the floozy to get lost, and dragged him back to her car.

"Where are we going?" he asked.

"Wherever the road leads us," she said, no clue what she was doing, only that she had to do *something*. She got on the highway and drove, trusting that God would help her figure things out.

At first, Jack was apologetic, saying he was sorry over and over, promising Susan that he'd never do it again.

She said nothing. Just kept driving.

His cries turned to anger, accusations that she didn't know what it was like for him — the pressure of his job, the soul-sucking nature of his work, and how she didn't understand him.

And she drove, feeling God pushing her forward.

Where am I going?

You'll know when you get there, she felt Him say.

Eventually, Jack fell asleep.

She drove until sunrise, finding herself on a long stretch of mountain road with nothing in sight but rocks and trees.

Then she came to a long bridge overlooking a lake far below.

She glanced to her right and saw orange bleeding into the violet sky, a sight so beautiful she had to stop.

She shook Jack awake, and they got out of the car.

Then, the floodgates opened.

Jack told her about his awful childhood, how his father had been a monster. How no matter how happy he was, Jack always felt like he wasn't deserving, that something, somehow would come along and destroy everything.

"You don't have to follow your father's footsteps," she told him. "You aren't him. You are a kind, loving man."

He held her tightly, sobbing.

It was the first time she'd ever seen him weep, and it made her cry right alongside him.

She told him she was pregnant.

He cried again. At first, she thought he was upset, but then realized they were tears of joy.

Because Jack had found God.

He promised never to let the darkness back inside.

As we pull up to the cabin, with Jack's Panamera outside, I fear that the darkness *has* returned. And it's up to me to help drive it out before he does something he'll regret forever, something that will destroy Ms. Valencia's life, *and* the Caldwell family.

Am I up to the task?

Waylon looks at me as we approach the door. "You sure you wanna go in there?"

"Yes."

He shrugs then sticks his keys in the lock and unlocks the door.

Jack appears before we've made it ten steps into the living room. A disheveled mess — shirt untucked, hair messy and sweaty, blood stains on his shirt, holding a bottle of whiskey.

"What are you doing here?" he asks, staring at us wild-eyed.

"What the hell are *you* doing?" Waylon says.

"You should go home, both of you." His voice is slurred, eyes red.

I hear a cry from a room somewhere in the back.

I start toward it.

Jack gets in my way.

"No."

"Let her go," I say.

"No. If the police aren't going to do their jobs, I will."

Waylon comes toward us. "Come on, Jack, you've gotta give them time. They only questioned her yesterday. They have to build a case before they can make an arrest."

"They ain't arresting her!" He takes a swig of whiskey. "We both know it."

I challenge him. "So, what, this is your idea of justice? Kidnapping her? Hurting her?"

A horrible thought occurs to me. What if Carla is dying? What if he has passed the point of no return?

"Please, tell me you didn't …" I can't finish voicing the thought, lest I somehow make it true.

Jack looks up at me with a sneer. And for a moment, I'm certain we're too late, that Carla is bleeding out.

Oh, God no.

Waylon pushes past Jack, heading toward the back of the cabin.

Jack goes to stop him, but he's not fast enough.

Seconds after he reaches the room in the back, Waylon cries out, "What did you do?"

I run after Waylon, also past Jack, and join him in the doorway. Carla is sitting in the chair, tied up, blood all over her clothes, face bruised purple, one cheek the size of a golf ball.

My gut drops as she looks up, eyes almost void of emotion.

I turn to Jack, now coming into the room, then run up and, with both hands balled into fists, shove him backward.

"What did you do?"

He stumbles back, somehow managing to stay on his feet.

"It's her fault Chelsea's in a coma! We trusted her. She's a teacher! And she took advantage of our girl, abused her trust. *She turned our little girl gay!* Chelsea's gonna burn in Hell for eternity because of her."

He breaks down, crying.

Waylon stares at me, speechless.

I remember how smooth he had been when talking to Jack, how he could pretty much handle any situation, spin it to their benefit.

How the hell is he gonna spin *this?*

I go over to Carla, fumble with her gag.

"What are you doing?" Jack calls out.

"I'm taking this thing off her before she chokes to death!"

I pull the gag off, and Carla looks up at me, her terrified eyes lighting with life — help is here.

"Please," she cries, "I need to see a doctor."

I look down, see blood soaking her blue top near her abdomen. I pull up at the bottom of her top, see a bandage soaked in blood.

She'll bleed out if we don't get her help.

I look back at Jack and see a knife on the floor.

"You stabbed her?"

He looks at me, nodding. "Yes, I was trying to get her to admit it."

"Admit what?"

"That Chelsea was only seventeen when she … abused her."

Oh, God.

I wonder if this is somehow *my* doing. I wonder if I somehow planted a seed of thought in Jack's head while in his body and the cops wanted me to get Carla to confess to seducing Chelsea before she was of age. I had tried to trick a confession out of her, but she didn't bite. Namely, because Chelsea wasn't seventeen at the time. *I* understood that, but apparently, Jack is still a victim of this other theory. Maybe it's because he isn't getting the full picture of my interpretations of data — his brain is left to create a sensible narrative. Unfortunately, the one that makes the most sense to him is that Carla is a monster who must pay for her sins. But first, he needs her to admit her wrong-doing so he can feel good about what he's done, or plans to do.

"We need to get her to a hospital," I say, eyes locked on Carla's, trying to get a sense of how coherent she is. Not that I'd know the signs of someone about to die from blood loss.

"I agree," Waylon says, coming over to my side and helps to untie her.

"Stop!" Jack says.

We're not listening.

Waylon is pulling at the knots as I kneel down to Carla's side and take her hand. "We're going to get you out of here."

"I said STOP!" Jack shouts.

His tone is so abrupt, we both turn.

He has a gun in his hands, aimed at us.

"She's not leaving."

"Whoa, what the hell are you doing, Jack?" Waylon raises his hands in that way you do to calm an unreasonable person.

"I'm not going to let her destroy this family. If she leaves, she'll go right to the cops and have me arrested."

My first thought is to say *yeah, of course she is, you whacko*. But I can't say that. I wouldn't have previously pegged Jack as the violent type, but that was before I knew he was a drunk. Alcohol can soak out everything you know about someone, make them capable of some truly heinous shit.

"You don't want to do this," I say, approaching him, my hands also raised.

He doesn't put the gun on me. It's still aimed past me, at Carla. As I step between them, blocking his aim, he moves to counter mine, determined not to surrender his shot.

My heart is racing. I'm picturing this going to hell. Maybe he'll aim at Carla and hit me, or Waylon. Tragedy in every direction.

"She's not going to the police," Waylon chimes in. "Are you, Ms. Valencia?"

She gives us all a groggy *No*.

Jack shakes his head, runs one of his hands through his sweat-mopped hair. "No, she's going to tell. She'll ruin us!"

"No," Waylon says. "We'll pay her off. Pay her to keep quiet on this. She's out of a job once the school finds out, right? She's got nothing, Jack. We can pay her to keep quiet. Pay her, and this all goes away. You with me, Ms. Valencia?"

She nods, crying. "Yes, I swear, I won't tell anyone. I just want this over. *Please*."

Jack swallows, glaring at Carla, gun trembling in his hand, lips a slit across his clenched jaw.

He shakes his head again. "No, someone's gonna find out. We can't just bring her to the hospital like this. Someone's gonna ask questions, and then what? The police will come looking for me. And I won't hold up to their questions. We've gotta end this now. You have people who can fix things, right, Waylon? People who can hide a body."

He doesn't wait for an answer.

Jack marches forward, eyes zeroed in on Carla, intent to finish her off.

I throw myself in front of Carla and grab the gun.

We struggle as I push his hands upward with the gun.

Jack's eyes widen, surprised I'm trying to stop him, or maybe of my strength.

"Let go," he hisses.

"No," I say, eyes locked on his. "I won't let you do this. Chelsea wouldn't want it."

His strength falters at the sound of her name.

His legs buckle.

He falls to his knees and releases the gun.

I slide the weapon to Waylon. He grabs it and shoves the gun into his waistband as if he's done so a hundred times. Then he grabs Carla and throws an arm around her, helping her to stand.

"I'm gonna take her. It's best you all don't come with me."

"Okay," I say, "I'll drive us back in Jack's car. Thank you, Waylon."

He nods.

"And I'm sorry, Carla." I meet her eyes. "We will make this up to you. I promise."

She stares at me, her eyes blank and expression numb.

They leave.

Jack is on the ground, sobbing in a heap.

I stare at him, my heart breaking for his pain, and for my part in this.

"I just want her back," he says. "I just want Chelsea back."

I kneel down beside him, put a hand on his shaking back, and hug him.

"We both do."

Together, we cry.

THE SUN HAS SET, and we're both lying on the ground, staring up at the ceiling.

I'm thinking about Chelsea, wondering why I'm here. Was it to save Carla? Was it to stop Jack from murder? Or is there a chance I can save Chelsea? Or, at the very least, find the person who set this nightmare in motion.

I turn to see Jack still staring up at the ceiling. He hasn't breathed a word since saying he just wanted Chelsea back.

He turns to me and says, "Do you still believe in God?"

I can't answer for myself. I don't know *what* I believe. But I know the answer he needs to hear. I know what Susan would say.

"Yes. More than ever."

"How? How can He let this happen to our little girl? Yes, she sinned, but no sinner deserves this hell."

"She needs us to be strong now more than ever. *I* need you to be strong."

He looks at me, reaches over, and wipes a tear from my cheek.

Jack is lost, in pain, and ashamed.

I need to help him find his shore so he can start swimming home.

"Do you want to go for a ride?" I ask.

"To where?"

"Wherever the road leads us."

He takes my hand, and together we stand.

Chapter Five

I WAKE up standing in a park.

I'm confused.

Something's not right, but I can't quite put my finger on what it is.

I never wake standing. I always find myself in someone as their body is waking up. Am I to believe that this body was asleep while standing?

Maybe they had an epileptic fit, and at the moment they were out, I slipped right in?

I look around. The park is empty, except for a pair of mothers jogging on a path, both pushing strollers with babies or toddlers, far from where I'm standing.

I'm between a soccer field and an empty playground. Well, not quite empty. There's a girl in a black hoodie sitting on the swing. I can't see her details from here. With her eyes on the ground, she appears to be a high school student, maybe killing time before school starts, or meeting a friend.

How did I get here?

Who am I?

I'm not getting anything.

This isn't right. I always get *something*. Even if I'm waking up as the world's biggest junkie, I get an indecipherable blur of memories at the very least.

But I don't feel drugged or otherwise incapacitated.

I look down at my hands and body. I'm a young woman, long dark hair, young-looking hands, pale skin. Maybe in my twenties?

There's a wooden pavilion with restrooms near the playground, along with some picnic tables and a water fountain. There's also a manager's office, though a metal gate over the window indicates that the manager isn't in.

I head toward the building. Maybe my host's reflection in the bathroom mirror will trigger something.

A cool breeze whips my hair as I break into a jog.

I push through the door and make my way to the row of five sinks and the long mirror hanging over them.

As I look up, a jolt of déjà vu.

I don't know who I am, but at the same time, I feel like I've seen this woman's face before — bright green-blue eyes, full lips, and bright pink cheeks. She looks so familiar, but I can't rem—

The bathroom door opens.

The girl from the swings walks in, pulls her hoodie back, and reveals another familiar face: *Chelsea!*

"What are you—" I start to ask, but she cuts me off.

"So, this is what you look like?"

"What?" I ask, confused. Does she know my host?

"Funny, I would've pictured you as a blonde."

"What are you talking about?" I ask.

"You, the woman who's been pretending to be all these people — me, my brother, my father, my mother."

"Wait, how do you — "

I have so many questions — I can't even get the words

out. How does she know I'm a Jumper? How is she even here? And why is she saying this is what I look like?

"Know who you are?" she finishes for me.

"Yeah," I say, staring at her as she stands just two feet away, staring right back at me.

This can't be real. A part of me wants to reach out and touch her, but I'm afraid to shatter the dream — if that's what this is — before it casts light on some great mystery.

"Ever since I went into a coma, I've been ... outside of myself. I wake, and I'm in my house. I wake again, and I'm somewhere else. No real control. But I kept waking up near my family, and I kept sensing you inside them. It's like I could see this shifting shape within them, like a cross between a ghost and a light. At first, you were in me — I remember sensing you as I woke up from my overdose. I could see my family around my bed, and I tried to tell them how sorry I was, but *you* were there. *You* were in control. And then you were in Billy, then my dad, and then Carla, and then my mom. And now you're here, a ghost like me, without someone else's body to hide inside."

"Of course I've got a body, I'm—"

And then I realize — this *is* my body, or maybe some a projection.

This is Ella.

I look back in the mirror, on the verge of tears.

"Oh, my God. I'm in *my* body."

"What are you, and what are you doing here, interfering in my life?" Chelsea asks me, her voice on the cusp of accusation.

"I'm not interfering. I'm trying to help you."

"*Help?*" she laughs. "You call driving my father to almost kill Carla help? Do you know how helpless I felt watching him do that to her? Watching him torture her?"

Now *she's* the one crying.

"I'm sorry. And to answer your question, I don't know what I am, or why I'm here."

Chelsea looks at me, eyebrow arched. "Bullshit."

"I swear. I've been waking up in a different body almost every day for the past year. And before then, I can't remember anything. I don't choose who I wake up in, nor do I know why any of this is happening to me."

I don't tell her about the assassins, or the weird messages I hear. That would only confuse or frighten her.

She stares at me, head tilted as if reading me.

"All I know is that the people I wake up in usually need some help, or I'm given a chance to save someone. I saved a girl from a serial killer a month or so ago. Maybe I'm here to save you."

"I didn't *ask* to be saved," Chelsea says, turning away, giving me the teenage angst that annoys me so much.

"Maybe it's not up to *you*."

"So, what, God sent you?"

I laugh. "I don't think it's God."

"Then what?"

"I don't know, but I do know that you don't *really* want to die. Why else would you still be hanging out here, popping up around your family? Why follow me into the bathroom? You're hanging on for a reason."

She doesn't look at me. Still, I know I'm right.

"You feel bad, especially now that all this has happened, to your parents, to your brother, to Carla."

She turns around. "She doesn't deserve this! Carla didn't *abuse* me. She didn't *make me gay*."

"I know. I was inside her. I know that she loves you."

"You can tell how people feel when you're in them?"

"Yes, especially strong emotions, like love."

"What was she thinking about me?"

"That she loves you and misses you. That she never

meant to fall in love, but now that she is, she's not sure how she can go on without you."

Chelsea wipes tears from her eyes. "What do I do? I don't know how to go back, how to wake back up in *my body*."

"I'm sorry. I don't know how any of this works. I don't even know how we're here together right now. In the past year I've been jumping, I've never even seen my own body, let alone someone in a coma. Have you ever had an out-of-body experience before?"

Chelsea stares past me, to the mirror. "I thought it was a dream at the time. I was six, maybe seven, and I was really sick. I don't know what I had, but my family was super-worried. My fever was through the roof. They brought me to the hospital. I was in the back seat on the way there. My mom was holding my head in her hands, and then suddenly I was gone. I was at my grandma's, my mom's mom, sitting in her tiny apartment, watching as she rocked in her chair, watching *Wheel of Fortune*. I tried talking to her, to ask her how I got there, but she didn't hear me. Then she stopped rocking, and I woke back up in the hospital. They said I'd been unconscious for fourteen hours until the fever broke. I didn't tell anyone about the dream where I went to Grandma's, but later that morning my mom got a call from her brother that she was dead."

"Oh, my. And you never told anyone?"

"Oh, no. My family would've thought it was witchcraft or the devil or something. They used to be a lot more hard-core in their Christianity if you can believe that. They didn't even let me read *Harry Potter* when I was a kid, because, *whoo, witches*. I didn't read the series until Carla lent me her copies."

"Do you think it's possible that you overheard your parents say something while you were unconscious, that maybe your brain made up the whole thing with your grandma to make sense of what you were hearing?"

"No, she didn't get the call until *after* I'd woken. I remember because she left the room, then came back in crying, and pulled Dad into the hall. They didn't want to tell me what was going on until I made them."

I stare at Chelsea, trying to make sense of what I can't understand.

"Okay, so you obviously have some ability to astral travel, or something. But why am *I* here, in the park with you? I've never been in this situation. I'm always in someone else's body. So, why am I here now?"

"I dunno," Chelsea shrugs. "I was hoping *you'd* have answers. Maybe you're here to help me get back to my body."

"If only I knew."

"Do you think Carla will be okay?"

I'm about to answer when I notice a sound, barely noticeable.

Chelsea repeats her question, but I hold up a finger. "Shh, do you hear that?"

"Hear what?"

I cup my hands to my ears. It doesn't make sense, as I'm not physically here, and therefore my hands shouldn't be able to amplify the sound to my ears, but using that logic, I wouldn't be able to hear anything. And I can hear something, like … *static*.

And then the sound of a woman's voice: "The women's restroom."

Oh, no.

My mind flashes to when The Collectors showed up the last time I saw the assassin. They'd come to eat my soul, she told me before shooting my host in the head to send it elsewhere and out of their reach. She'd saved me, why I don't know, but what if they haven't stopped looking for me?

"I've gotta go," I say.

"What? Where?"

"I don't know. There are these things after me, Collectors. They eat souls."

I spot a long row of windows above the toilets.

I step into a stall, climb onto the toilet seat, and hoist myself up enough to peek out the window.

There, in the center of the soccer field, I see the two mothers who were jogging with their carriers. They're just standing there, staring at us. The carriers are on the jogging path, children abandoned, oblivious that something has taken over their mothers' bodies.

The Collectors look up and see me, and as they do so, their faces blur and refocus.

Oh, shit!

They start walking toward us.

"Oh, God!" I scramble down from the toilet and run up to Chelsea, putting both of my hands on her shoulders.

"What?" Chelsea asks, her eyes panicked.

"They're here!"

"The Collectors?"

Something else occurs to me. What if they're not here for me? What if they're here for Chelsea? Come to collect her stray soul?

"Yes. Can you get us out of here?"

"I don't know how I got here! I just show up places. I don't have any control!" Chelsea cries, her voice rising in pitch.

"Maybe you do. Maybe *you* brought me here. I need you to try. Think yourself somewhere else. Maybe think *both of us* somewhere else."

"How? I don't know what to do!"

"Close your eyes, imagine us somewhere else. Anywhere else!"

I run back to the toilet and peek through the window. The Collectors are closing in, maybe thirty yards away. They're not running, and it's almost scarier that they're not. They're walking straight toward us, no doubt that they'll catch us.

I wonder if we should try to run, but something stops me from suggesting it. I don't know if it's instinct or fear, but I have a feeling that we'll never get away if we run. Somehow, these things will catch us.

"Lock the door!" I yell.

Chelsea runs to the door and flips the lock. I wonder how she turned it, or, for that matter, how I opened the door if our bodies aren't really here. Is it some form of energy we're exerting, even without a physical shell? Or are souls somehow able to interact with objects? I feel like I'm trying to figure out ghost logic, but I can't stop to consider any of this now. I need to help her focus, to try and teleport us somewhere else — away from those things.

She comes to me as I back out of the stall.

"What do we do now?"

"Keep trying to think us somewhere else."

"How?"

"Close your eyes, think of somewhere you've been. Think of the details, imagine them so real you can almost touch them."

Suddenly, I have another idea.

"No, forget that. Focus on someone you have a strong emotional connection to."

"Like Carla?"

"Yes, like Carla."

The door shakes in its frame, someone trying to open it.

No, not someone, *something*.

Chelsea's eyes are wide, terrified. "Oh, God."

"Just focus," I tell her.

The door shakes harder.

Now pounding.

The Collectors don't speak. Or demand entry. They just act.

They're pounding on the door. The handle is rattling.

The way the door is moving in its frame, The Collectors must be stronger than the women they occupy.

Can they break down a door? And once they do, what will happen? Will they take my soul? Or Chelsea's?

The assassin said that I'm dead if they catch me. *Worse than dead*, whatever that means.

We've got to get out of here. *Now.*

Chelsea is squeezing her eyes shut, crying. "I can't."

I look at the door, shaking harder. Grunts come from the other side — animalistic sounds from demons determined to get to us.

I look at Chelsea. Her eyes are wide open, staring at the door. She can't focus.

I reach out and put my hand on her cheek.

Startled, she looks away from the door, and toward me.

"Think about the painting you made for Carla. She still has it. She's waiting for you to finish. You need to finish it, Chelsea. You *will* finish it."

The door breaks open.

And in an instant, Chelsea vanishes.

I turn to see The Collectors storming the restroom.

Chapter Six

I WAKE WITH A GASP, startled and relieved to find myself in a teenage boy's dark and messy bedroom.

She got away.

We got away.

But I wonder if and when The Collectors might come searching for me again. I escaped them the first time only because the assassin killed my host. But killing the host isn't an option for me. I can't kill innocent people just to escape these Collectors.

I'm not sure how I escaped this time. The only thing that makes sense is that Chelsea somehow brought me there, and once she was gone, my reason for being went with her, and I was sent to wherever my body goes when I'm out of a host.

So, I escaped. Again.

But what happens when they come for me when I'm in the body of a little kid or someone's parent? It's not like I can fall asleep on command. Given that those are the only ways I know of jumping to another body, I feel trapped like a hunted animal, without any means to fight back.

I look at the clock and see that it's five after noon on Sunday. I didn't miss a day. I went from being Susan on Saturday to waking up early Sunday as myself, and now I'm waking again, this time back in a body. Not just any body, but Anthony Rocco.

I sit up, excited that maybe this is the chance I've been waiting for — a chance to find out who the hell black-mailed Chelsea into making that video.

I get out of bed, step over piles of dirty clothes, books, and video game boxes, and find Rocco's iPhone sitting on a desk littered with pornographic pictures that look printed from his computer, empty Mountain Dew cans, and a half-eaten box of pizza sitting wide open.

Wonderful.

Doesn't this kid have parents? In every other teenage boy I've been in, they've at least made an attempt — half-assed as it might have been — to hide their pornography. But Rocco leaves his right out in the open. And not even the tame stuff, but hardcore smut that looks borderline illegal.

I sit back down on the bed and swipe his phone.

It's password protected, but the password comes instantly to mind.

I'm in.

I find a text thread between him and Blake Wellington starting back from forever ago.

I start thumbing backward, looking for anything mentioning Chelsea or the video.

A recent text from Blake says:

Yo, maybe you should delete some of that shit. A lot of heat might be coming down with this suicide attempt.

∾

Rocco responded:

∾

Already done.

∾

But as I thumb back and find the beginning of the conversation, I realize he lied.

∾

The first message is from Blake, and it says:

∾

Yo, Rocco, look at good lil bible girl.

   Seems like she's not such a "good girl" after all, is she? More like a big slut!

   P.S. Now you owe me.

   Attached: Good_Christian_Slut.mov

∾

The preview thumbnail shows Chelsea in that dark room as she lost everything to these sick fucks.

And it wasn't Rocco. Blake was the one who had been blackmailing her. After that it's a back-and-forth between the jocks, laughing, saying how "surprisingly hot" she is, and debating whether or not she's any good in bed. Later in the thread, Rocco asked:

~

How did you get her to do all that freaky shit?

Blake: LOL. The ladies love me.

Rocco: No, for realz.

Blake: Let's just say I recorded her and a certain dyke art teacher licking each other.

Rocco: NO WAY!

Blake: Yup. And I told her if she didn't put on a show for me, I'd send it to everyone. Maybe even to her Daddy, or the news.

Rocco: MUST SEE DYKE VIDEO.

Blake: No. I promised her I'd delete it.

Rocco: No way you deleted it! Bullshit.

Blake: Maybe, maybe not.

Rocco: Trade?

Blake: What you got?

Rocco: Okay, here. Attached: drunksex_Becca.mov

~

I CLICK on the thumbnail and immediately wished that I hadn't.

It's Rocco coercing some drunk girl into sex, recording the whole thing from a hidden camera focused on his bed.

I can't see her face, just from her chest down. She's in a shirt and skirt, but not for long. He's taking them off.

She's resisting, but he's not taking no for an answer.

Soon, he's between her legs.

She's barely conscious, but he doesn't care. Hell, that might be what makes it so thrilling.

This is rape!

I've seen enough of the video, but then, just as I'm about to turn it off, her face comes into frame, and I realize it's *that Becca*, the redhead who told me that Chelsea was sleeping with the teacher.

She seemed nicer than the others in her crew. She also seemed so uncomfortable telling me that news.

And I realize — they made her tell me. They *wanted* the student-teacher affair to get out there, maybe to take the focus off the video.

Those fuckers.

In response to the Becca video, Blake wrote:

~

AWESOME. Keep 'em cumming. And maybe I'll send you the dyke on dyke action.

~

ROCCO SENT him eight more videos, each with a different girl's name.

No. These can't all be him. Can they?

I click on the first one, and it's the same setting and scene as the Becca video. As are the next three.

I can't watch any more.

These people are monsters.

Later in the thread, Blake texts, pissed.

~

BLAKE: Did you upload the Chelsea shit to porn sites?
Rocco: Wasn't me.
Blake: Nobody else has the video!
Rocco: It wasn't me!
Rocco: Oh, shit, I bet it was Kris.

❧

KRIS IS a cheerleader fuck buddy of Rocco's.

❧

BLAKE: What? You showed Kris?

Rocco: No, I didn't SHOW her. She saw it on my computer and asked what the hell it was. Thought I was sleeping with Chelsea. I told her no, someone sent it to me.

Blake: You had it on your computer?

Rocco: Kinda hard to jerk off on a phone video. Too small, so I sent it to my computer. And she was over here using it for her report. She laughed, calling Chelsea a fucking hypocrite. But I had no idea she was gonna upload it to a porn site! I swear!

Rocco: U mad?

❧

BLAKE DIDN'T RESPOND until a few days ago when he made the comment about erasing the texts because the heat would be on them.

If Blake ever sent the video of Chelsea and her teacher, it wasn't on Rocco's phone. But there are a ton of other videos on there, all with different girls' names.

Did he rape all these girls?

Pretty ballsy, or damn stupid, not to delete any of them, especially after Blake told him that shit might get hot with Chelsea's suicide attempt.

I'm getting some memories indicating that Rocco was hanging on to the Chelsea video and the texts as leverage against Blake, in case Blake ever decided to fuck with him.

The blackmailer getting blackmailed over his blackmail video.

Seems appropriate, even if I'm disgusted by both of these scumbags.

I have to do something. I've got the evidence to nail both of these monsters and put them away for a long time.

Suddenly, I hear a girl say, "Gross!"

I look up and see Chelsea, standing right in front of Rocco's bed, looking at his disgusting decor.

"Chelsea! It's me, Ella. I'm in Rocco's body!"

"Yeah, I can see you. What happened? Last thing I knew I was thinking of Carla. I wound up in a doctor's office with her and Waylon, but I don't think it was a normal office because doctors aren't usually open on Sundays, right?"

"No, it's probably someone Waylon knows. Is she okay?"

"I think so. What happened to you? Did those Collectors get a hold of you?"

"I don't think so. I vanished right after you, then woke up here, in *paradise*."

Chelsea laughs.

It's good to hear her laugh.

"How did you find me?"

"I just thought of you, and I wound up here."

"Wow. So you can control it now?"

"Maybe. Or maybe I got lucky twice. I don't wanna mess around too much and wind up somewhere I don't want to be, or lost without a way to get back."

"I understand. Listen, I found out who coerced you into making that … *video*." It feels weird to mention the video to Chelsea, like I'm violating her just by talking about it, and, of course, by having seen it.

"Who?" she asks, eyes wide, waiting for an answer.

"Blake Wellington."

She stares at me for a long moment, and I'm not sure

if she's in disbelief, shock, or some other emotion I can't quite decipher. I wait for her to speak.

I fill her in on everything I found out, how Rocco was raping several girls and filming it, how Kris probably uploaded Chelsea's video to some porn site, and how Blake admitted to the whole thing in his texts.

She's still staring, no expression.

"This is good news," I say. "We've got them. I can walk into the police station right now and turn in this phone with enough evidence to put Rocco and Blake away."

"No," she says.

"What?"

"They'll get off."

"What do you mean they'll get off? This is evidence of blackmail, extorting a sex video, and God knows how many rapes Rocco committed."

"You don't know how this town works. Their parents will find a way to get them off. They'll pay off witnesses, experts, or something. Rocco's father is a lawyer for criminals; it's his job to get scumbags off on technicalities or bribe jurors."

I'm not sure how she can possibly know they bribe jurors, or if she's just overly dramatic.

"And Blake's dad will never let his son do time. Never. It won't happen. Blake had an older brother who was in a hit and run, was totally drunk, killed a family of three, and he never saw a day behind bars. You think a blackmail video will get him locked up? It's his word against mine. And when it comes right down to it, he didn't put a gun to my head. I *could've* said no."

Her eyes are welling up, and it suddenly occurs to me that maybe, in some twisted way, Chelsea thinks she deserves what happened. Maybe that's partly why she tried to kill herself. I want to ask, but I'm afraid if I'm wrong, I'll only hurt her feelings.

"He forced you. He used a video he took of you, probably also illegal, to coerce your performance. That's illegal as hell, and there's no way any jury could see otherwise."

"You're assuming I'll ever wake up to testify. Maybe this is it for me — doomed to walk the earth as a ghost forever. Maybe this is God's sentence for trying to kill myself, or for being a lesbian. Maybe this is karma for all the shit I caused Carla to go through."

I stand, put my hands on her shoulders, and meet her eyes.

She can barely look at me.

I'm not sure if it's because I'm in the body of one of her tormentors, or if she doesn't want to hear reason.

"First of all, God didn't punish you for being a lesbian. That's bullshit, okay? I don't care what holy book says what, those books were written by men with agendas. You *have* to know that."

"I don't know what I know anymore."

"Second of all, Carla is a grown woman. She should've been more cautious. Yeah, I get it, she loves you, but still, it's on her more than you. You're just a kid."

"I'm eighteen. Not a kid."

She's starting to fight back a bit. Good.

"I'm going to the police station and turning Rocco and Blake in."

"It won't work!"

"We don't know unless we try."

"I have a better idea," she says, finally meeting my gaze.

"What?"

"I want you to stop them so they can never do this to anyone else."

"That's what I'm going to do."

"No," she says. "Really stop them."

"Are you saying you want me to … kill them?"

She nods.

"No, I can't do that."

"Why?"

"I don't kill innocent people."

"They're *innocent?*"

"Well, no, they're not innocent, but it's not up to me to decide if they live or die. That's why you have laws."

She pauses for a moment, eyebrow arched. "Wait a second, what do you mean you 'don't kill innocent people?' Are you saying you've killed others? *Guilty* ones?"

Shit, I was afraid she caught that.

I let out a deep sigh.

"You have, haven't you?" Her grin is huge.

She hops onto the bed, sitting cross-legged. "Tell me."

Well, I have wanted someone to confide in, and this is the first person to come along that's in a similar situation, at least one who isn't an assassin.

I tell her everything.

Once I'm done, she's staring at me again, but this time not in shock. Judging from the small smile teasing the corners of her mouth, I think she's admiring me.

"Don't you see? This is why you're here! You were meant to kill them. Why else would you be in Rocco's body, one of the few people in Blake's inner circle who could slit his throat or something?"

"I don't know. It doesn't feel right."

She stares at me, arms crossed, "It feels freaking *perfectly right* to me. Hell, I'd say it's almost karmic! You were meant to be here, to do this. For me."

"Killing them won't change what happened to you, or

Carla. And it won't bring you back. It might even make you feel worse."

"I can't possibly feel worse than the way they made me feel."

"You say that, but you don't know it. Thinking about killing someone and doing it are two very different things. You have to live with it forever. *I* have to live with it forever."

My phone rings.

I look at the screen and see Blake's name.

Chelsea sees it and looks at me. "See? Fate!"

I pick up the phone.

"Yeah?" I say, figuring that's how Rocco would answer his phone. I avoid the urge to add a grunt, even though I'm pretty sure it would crack Chelsea up.

"You ready?"

"Ready for what?"

"Dude, don't tell me you forgot!"

I pretend to sound like I'm just waking up, stalling for time until Rocco's memories fill me in on what it is I'm supposed to be doing with Blake. I'm guessing it's not going to church.

Then I remember: a fishing trip on his new boat. Just the two of us.

"Nah, I'm just fucking with you. Gimme a few minutes to freshen up."

"Freshen up?" There's no way Rocco would say "freshen up." He'd say "take a shower" or "wash my nuts." Something more macho.

"Did you grow a pussy overnight?"

"You wish."

"Well, hurry the hell up, I'm outside in your driveway. Tell your maid to open the door and let me in."

There's no way I want to put him in the same room as

Chelsea. No, he probably can't see her, but I'm pretty sure she'll lose it if she sees him.

"I'll be right out," I say.

"You sure you don't want to *freshen up?*"

"Fuck you," I say and hang up the phone.

I look up to find Chelsea is gone.

~

IT'S A BEAUTIFUL COOL, crisp day in the middle of nowhere.

We're sitting in Blake's new boat — a present from Daddy for being a douche, I assume — in the center of Lake Harrison, with nothing but water and trees for as far as I can see in every direction. I can see the shore about twenty minutes away if I squint, along with Blake's pickup and trailer.

There's an open tackle box at my feet, and inside is a big fat knife practically begging me to stick it in Blake.

I can't help but wonder if Chelsea is right. It sure as hell feels like Fate *wants* me to kill this spoiled rich bastard.

Blake is sitting in his seat in the bow, fishing pole in one hand, beer in the other. We haven't caught anything, but I guess that isn't the point of fishing with these two. It's been mostly talking about football, chicks, and cars, topics I'm not exactly well-versed in. Fortunately, Rocco practically lives and breathes all three of those things, so responses are floating like low hanging fruit in his mind. Easy pickings, so long as I don't overdo it and get too technical. It's easy to talk with Blake since 90 percent of the conversation is him going on and on about these things. I think maybe he's only friends with Rocco because the guy never disagrees, is an eager audience, and practically reveres him.

Hell, if I didn't know better, I'd think Rocco has a bit of a crush on his friend.

Blake looks back at me, as if he senses something's off. He lifts his shades, and his blue eyes pierce through me.

"Aren't you gonna drink, man? What's wrong with you?"

"Yeah, sure." I lean forward from my spot in the center of the boat and dip my hands into the cooler full of ice, imported beer, and a few plastic bottles of water.

I grab a Heineken, even though I have no interest in drinking, and take a swig.

"There ya go." Blake lowers his shades and gives me the charming grin he's honed to perfection.

Chelsea's voice startles me from behind. "Ask him about me."

I jump up and drop the Heineken, nearly sending my pole into the lake.

"Shit, dude, what the fuck?" Blake asks, startled by my surprise.

"Sorry, I thought I saw something."

Not the best response.

"You did see something," Chelsea says. "Me."

I turn to see her smiling.

"Oh, look," she says, leaning over and looking into the tackle box, "a knife! How convenient!"

I want to tell her to go away, to shut up, but then I'd be talking to myself, and Blake will be on the defensive.

I grab the Heineken, having only spilled a bit, and take a quick drink.

Blake is looking at me. It's hard to read his expression from behind the shades.

"So, what did you see?"

"Huh?"

"You said you thought you saw something, what did you think you saw? The Loch Ness Monster?"

I laugh, probably too forced, surely too nervous.

"No, just like a shadow or something. Ever see a shadow out of the corner of your eyes and it startles you?"

"Yeah, I guess." He shrugs, then turns his attention to his line in the water, watching the bobber dip.

He sets down his drink and reels in the line to tighten it. The bobber dips down and reels faster.

Then the line goes slack.

"Shit!" he says, pulling in the now-empty hook. "Had a bass at least two feet wide."

He digs into a Styrofoam container of worms, baits his hook again, and casts his line.

"Ask him about me," Chelsea repeats.

I look back at her, noticing that even though a nice cool breeze is blowing through Rocco's hair, hers is unfazed by the wind.

I mouth the word, *fine.*

"I don't know," I begin, "I've been spooked ever since Chelsea tried to kill herself."

"Hmmph," Blake says.

No other comment?

I look back at Chelsea, who yells, "Is that it, you fuck? *Hmmph?* Fuck you!"

I really wish she'd vanish, maybe spend some time with Carla.

"Do you think about her?" I ask.

"Who? Bible Girl?"

"Yeah. Do you think about her, or what we did?"

"What *we did?*" he hasn't turned to look at me, which I find interesting. Is he suspicious of my line of questioning? I probably *do* sound like I'm wearing a wire. I should probably tone it down.

I turn back to Chelsea. She's staring at Blake, awaiting his answer.

I push further. "I dunno, I feel bad. I mean, I know I didn't want that video to get out there like that. I didn't tell Kris to do it, but she did, and then, I dunno, shit just snow-balled. Everyone seeing it and bullying her."

"Bullying her?" Blake spins around and glares at me through shades. "Boo-fucking-hoo. Some people called her a slut; so fucking what? She *was* a slut. If you don't want to be called a slut, don't be one! What, and now you feel sorry for her?"

"I am not a slut!" Chelsea stands up and yells with her fists at her sides like an angry little girl, though it does no good.

"Well, yeah, I kind of feel sorry for her. I mean, we ruined her life."

Blake laughs, takes off his shades, and sets his fishing pole down. "Let me get this straight, the dude who gets girls drunk or slips them GHB and rapes them, records it on video no less, is worried that we made a Christian hypocrite slut sad? Wow, this is rich! Maybe you *did* grow a pussy!"

"You're right. I'm a hypocrite. I didn't see it until someone tried to kill themselves because of shit we did."

Blake stands. "What are you saying, Rocco?"

"I'm turning myself in. I think you should do the same."

Blake looks like someone smacked him. His smile is gone, replaced with something stone cold sinister, devoid of life.

Is this a peek behind the sociopath's mask?

"The hell I will."

He's starting toward me.

What the hell is he going to do, start a fight in the boat?

He gets right in my face, so close I can feel the hot air from his nostrils on my skin.

His blue eyes are now two icy marbles, staring right through my skull. "I strongly suggest you reconsider."

"No," I say.

"Give me your phone."

"No."

He shoves me back.

I stumble and fall.

Chelsea screams, reaching out to smack him, but her hand goes right through his body. How can she lock a bathroom door, but not hit a person?

Blake is on me in a second, reaching into my jacket pocket and grabbing the phone before I can stop him.

He seizes it, stands up, and chucks it into the water.

"What the hell?" I yell.

He turns back to me, glaring. "I just saved you from fucking yourself."

"No, you're saving yourself."

Blake laughs. "You think my dad would let me get railroaded over some fucking video where some slut is spreading herself for me? Really? He'd have the state's best lawyers, better lawyers than your dad, make that shit disappear faster than a donut at a Weight Watchers meeting. No, Rocco, I'm saving *you*. Because you think your father can save you from a dozen or two rape charges? Maybe one or two, dude, but not that many."

I stare at Blake, weighing my next move. I don't think he's truly looking out for Rocco's interests. He's pretending to, but in reality, he's hoping that Rocco won't turn them in. Maybe he's right, maybe his father will get him off, but there's no way his reputation survives a scandal like this.

His body is tense, and for the first time, I'm sure Blake poses a serious threat to Rocco.

Chelsea is standing silently to my side, watching, glaring at him so hard she probably wishes she could grab the knife herself.

I have to play him like he's playing me.

I look down at the water, solemnly, almost ashamed to look at him. "You're right, man. I'm sorry. I just … I don't know. I feel like that bitch's ghost is following me around or something, making me feel like shit."

Blake sits down across from me, the tackle box, and the blade inside it, close enough for him to grab if he wanted.

I don't even look at the box, staring at the water instead.

Blake says, "This shit has got you feeling guilty, man. It's okay. We didn't make Chelsea try and kill herself. She was a confused girl. Embarrassed about her affair with Ms. Valencia, afraid of what her Christian Daddy would say. That's why she OD'd. This shit would've gotten out with or without us, believe me. A student-teacher scandal always gets out, man. You watch the fucking news, all these MILFs fucking teenage boys. It's an epidemic, man, and this is the same, except this time with two dykes. But shit would've leaked, *with or without us.*"

I finally meet his eyes. "Yeah. I'm sorry."

He gives me that fake grin that gets him whatever he wants, including a Get Out of Jail Free card.

My blood boils as I realize that Chelsea, and even Blake, is right. He won't pay for what he did. Not ever. Yeah, I could probably turn Rocco in and still get him locked up, even without the videos on his phone, but Blake will go free no matter what.

That's just how it is.

He offers his hand to help me stand.

"We good, Bro?"

I take his hand.

As he pulls me up, I grab the knife from the tackle box. He doesn't even notice.

He pulls me up, and I slide the blade into his gut.

"Yeah, we're good," I say, driving the knife up into his lungs.

His eyes go wide.

He reaches out for my throat but doesn't have the strength to mount a defense.

I drive the blade deeper, pushing forward, fueled by rage.

I move closer, eyes now boring into his. I'm so close he can feel my breath on his face as I say, "This is for Chelsea."

I slide the knife diagonally, spilling Blake's guts onto the floor of his shiny new boat.

I watch as his body drops.

"Fuck yeah!" Chelsea yells.

She grabs me into a big hug, "Thank you, thank you, thank you!"

I hug her back, but all I can do is stare at the corpse, feeling almost like I'm outside of my — or rather Rocco's — body.

I killed someone I didn't need to kill. Someone who wasn't an immediate threat.

And … *it felt good.*

Chelsea pulls away to look at me. "Are you okay?"

"Yeah, I'm just going to go turn myself in and confess to killing Blake. If that doesn't put Rocco behind bars, I don't know what will."

She looks at me.

"Or you could not take any chances, and kill him too."

I stare at Blake's corpse, blue eyes staring up at the sun.

"No, I don't think I can. Sorry."

"It's okay," she says, embracing me again.

Her hug feels good, like a sister going through this hell, displaced beside me.

"Besides," I add, "If I turn Rocco in, I can confess to all these rapes. Maybe give these girls closure."

She doesn't say anything, just keeps her arms wrapped tightly around me.

Finally, she pulls away, meets my eyes, and in what feels like a *goodbye*, says, "What happens next? Will I see you again?"

"I don't know. Just think of me, I guess. But wait a day or so. I don't want you getting stuck in jail."

She laughs.

It feels so good to hear it.

Chapter Seven

I WAKE up in Billy's body.

I'm not sure why I'm still with this family, but there's a small comfort in the thought that I am, and that maybe I'll see his sister in ghostly travels again.

Now that Blake is dead and I confessed — as Rocco, to the murder, to the rapes, and how we conspired to ruin Chelsea's life — I'm betting that Rocco is waking up wondering about the fuck bomb dropped on his life. Before turning myself in, I recorded myself on Blake's phone confessing to his murder, and I even posed with his corpse a bit, to give the jury something to think about when considering his guilt. I'm guessing I've screwed him so hard he'll have to cop a plea, but even then, I can't imagine he'll get out quickly. Plus, he'll be persona non grata in this town, especially if Blake's father somehow maintains his power.

My bedroom door opens.

Billy's mom peeks in. "You awake?"

"Yeah," I say as my eyes adjust to the light bleeding in from the hallway.

"Come on. We've gotta take a ride."

"What is it?"

"You'll see."

A half hour later, we're pulling up to the hospital, and my heart begins to race.

The whole ride, Billy's mom and dad could hardly contain their happiness. Chelsea must have come out of her coma.

I ask, but they tell me to wait.

It's the first time I've seen either of them happy since I woke up in Chelsea's body. Is it possible that this family can heal? That they can overcome all of the hell that they've been through? If Chelsea is out of her coma, what's next? Will they allow her to see Carla again? Will Carla ever be able to forgive Jack Caldwell for his torture?

So many unknowns, but as we get out of the car and head through the hospital entrance, I dare to hope for a happy ending. If anyone deserves it, it's Chelsea.

We take the elevator to her floor and get out. I can't contain my excitement. I run toward her room, leaving Billy's parents behind.

I open the door and see Chelsea, her eyes open, smiling at me.

"Billy," she says, her voice still frail.

"Chelsea!" I run up and hug her, careful not to mess with any of the wires running from the machines to her bed, tears streaming down my cheeks.

Jack and Susan join in the hug.

"Thank you, Jesus," Jack says, "for bringing my little girl back."

Susan is crying. "Oh, honey, I thought we lost you."

"Not that easily," Chelsea says.

And just like that, everything feels almost normal.

We talk; well, mostly Jack and Susan talk. Chelsea

doesn't seem like she's pissed at Jack for what he did. She's acting as if things are okay. I wonder if she remembers.

After a bit, Chelsea asks if she can talk to me alone.

Jack and Susan look at her, surprised.

I put on my best innocent smile.

"Okay," Jack says. "Do you need anything? Want me to get some ice water or something?"

"That would be nice," she says.

They leave.

I look at Chelsea, wondering what she'll say to Billy. Will she tell him how much she missed him, maybe thank him for defending her?

The door swings closed. With Jack and Susan out of earshot, she whispers, "Thank you, Ella."

"You can—" I start to say *see me*, but stop. Of course she can.

"Yes, I can see you. Thank you for coming back."

"Like I said, I don't get to choose where I go."

"I'm still glad to see you, for real."

I hug her.

We talk some more, mostly her asking questions about what happened after I turned Rocco in, then a bit about what I think will happen with Carla and her father.

As the door starts to open, and her parents step inside, Chelsea squeezes my hand and says, "Thank you" again.

At lunchtime, the doctor comes to take her away for some tests.

Jack suggests we all head to an Italian restaurant nearby, then return in a few hours when Chelsea can receive visitors again.

We get into the elevator along with a doctor and an elderly couple who are talking so loud to one another despite being in such a confined space. What are the odds that both of their hearing aids are on the fritz?

The elevator doors close, and I feel a sudden uneasiness that I can't explain.

I look at Billy's parents. They're holding hands and smiling. Nothing like a little kidnapping and torturing of your child's teacher/lover to spice up a marriage, I guess.

I hear the faintest sound of static.

Oh, no. Not now.

My heart racing, I strain to hear a woman's voice relaying instructions, but the elderly couple turns every sound to mush.

As the black square above the doors counts down to ground level, the static grows louder.

No. No. No.

The Collectors have found me and are coming to collect my soul. They know I won't kill a child to escape them.

The doors will open, and there they'll be, their blank eyes somehow staring right through me. Then they'll …

The elevator doors open.

The static crackles and is replaced by the dulcet tones of Kenny G. coming over the elevator's tinny speakers.

We step outside the box, and I'm relieved to find that no one is waiting.

"You okay?" Jack asks.

I look up at him. "I am now."

Chapter Eight

O̶ne S̶aturday later

❧

THE LAST WEEK has been foggy, as if it means nothing.

All that matters is that I'm back in Chelsea's body.

I'm not sure where she is now, though I can feel her more than I've ever felt anyone else. I can feel her with me, though I'm not sure if she's aware of my presence. She's not talking to me like the ghost who met me in the bathroom or the girl who talked to me when she came out of her coma — yet she's here just the same.

I feel odd inside her with this awareness that she may be feeling me as much as I'm feeling her.

I spent most of the morning with her family, all of them in Recovery Mode — that odd space between forgiveness and moving on. They're on eggshells around me. Overly nice. I wonder if they're afraid I'll overdose again or wondering if they'll drive me back into Carla's arms.

From what I can tell, mostly from what I've overheard, as nobody is specifically discussing the matter with me, Waylon paid Carla off, so she won't be pressing charges. In exchange, he found a way to make sure that student-teacher affair stayed behind closed doors, and that the investigation never leaked, at least not through any official channels. Of course, Waylon couldn't stop every whisper, but Carla's face and name wouldn't be splashed all over the evening news for the muckraking journalists and vultures lying in wait for their nightly feast of misery to prey upon.

After lunch, I tell Mom and Dad that I need some fresh air, and want to take a drive.

Jack starts to say something. Maybe he wants to warn me away from Carla's, but then he catches himself and says, "Be careful."

I kiss them both on the cheek, then head out the door.

I drive aimlessly for a while, knowing where I *want* to go, but not sure if it's a good idea.

I go anyway.

I knock on Carla's door, anxiously awaiting her response.

What the hell am I doing here?

This is a terrible idea.

However, *I* — and not just Chelsea — can't shake the feeling of needing to see her and find out if she's okay.

The door eventually opens a crack, security chain in place.

Carla's eyes meet mine, but her expression isn't joy, or even surprise to see me alive and out of my coma. She's clearly terrified.

"What are you doing here?" Her voice is slightly changed from the still-swollen cheek. A violet bruise has swallowed the skin beneath her left eye. I'm almost afraid to know how many other injuries she suffered at Jack's hands.

"I wanted to see if you're okay."

"I'm fine. Please go."

"I am *soooo* sorry about what my dad did to you. He had no right. He — "

"Stop."

"What?" I ask.

She still hasn't unlatched the security chain.

"Please, I don't want to do this."

"Do what?" I ask, genuinely confused.

"Your father was right."

"What? No, he wasn't. Nobody should have to endure what you went through."

"Maybe, but I understand. He was afraid. He needed someone to blame, and he was right — I should never have let *this* go as far as it did. You were my student, and I knew better."

Chelsea's emotions are gushing forth in an unbridled wash of sorrow and deep, pining love. I can hardly control what comes out of my mouth.

"But I love you."

I'm shocked as it leaves my lips, but there are no take-backs.

This gets to Carla.

Her eyes are welling up, and she's quiet, maybe wondering if she should take the chain off the door and invite me inside.

"Please, don't give up on us. I'll make my father understand."

Carla stares at me, her chin quivering, resolve about to break. She's going to unchain the lock and open the door.

"They made me sign papers."

"What?" I ask.

"Made me sign papers that I wouldn't go to the police, news, or anybody else about what happened, and … "

Carla pauses as if unsure whether she should tell me the rest.

"And what?"

"And I can't see you anymore."

"And you signed?" I'm incredulous. Angry. "*Why*?"

"I just want this over. It's too much. And you don't need this in your life."

"Don't tell me what I need in my life. I know what I need — you."

She shakes her head. "Sorry, Chels. I just can't."

"Nobody has to know. And what's the worst thing that can happen if Dad *does* find out? The police already investigated you. You didn't break any laws. Hell, if anything, you have something on him — *he kidnapped and nearly killed you!*"

Carla shakes her head. "Sorry."

I feel a cold, dark anger.

"How much did he pay you?"

"What?" Carla asks, balking at the accusation.

"How much did he pay you?"

"It's not about the money."

"I want to know."

"Why?"

I can't stop the words spilling from my mouth. They're Chelsea's feelings, and there's nothing I can do to stop them.

"I want to know what I'm worth to you. What it's worth to throw my love away."

"It's not the money. I'm doing this for you."

"But I love you." Tears are streaming down my face, knife piercing my heart as if it were *me* Carla was rejecting rather than Chelsea.

94

"I love you, too," she says, "which is why I'm closing the door."

And then she does.

⌇

I STAND outside Carla's door, crying for what feels like an eternity.

I want to knock on her door, hell, bang on it, and demand that she see me. I know I can convince her that Jack will come around. He'll have to. I'll make him.

I know this is what Chelsea feels, but there's a part of me that feels this too. Have Chelsea's feelings somehow become mine? Am I that vested in their relationship that its collapse is killing me as if it were my own doomed love?

I can't commit Chelsea to this course of action.

If she wants to push this relationship while back in her body, fine, but it can't come from me.

It *must* be her.

I'm tired of screwing up my hosts' lives.

And so I leave Carla's porch.

Epilogue

IT'S BEEN ALMOST a month since I left the Caldwell family's circle. Today I'm a 60-year-old cab driver in Oregon named Martin O'Leary.

Usually, this far out from an event, memories get fuzzy, and it's hard to remember anything but a few details, shadows of people's lives.

But this time is different.

As I Jump from body to body, I keep finding myself wondering how Chelsea and Carla are doing. Did they get back together? Is their father keeping them apart? Surprisingly, their affair hasn't made the news.

I've never seen a story that scandalous just drop off the map, never even appearing in the headlines or gossip sites. It's as if someone scrubbed the story from existence. Did the kids at Chelsea's school feel sorry for her once Anthony Rocco and Blake Wellington's misdeeds came to light?

There was news about that, and a few mentions of Chelsea coming out of her coma. But the Caldwells and Carla have otherwise stayed under the radar. They've even deleted their social media accounts, so I can't check up on them that way.

Chelsea's father lost his TV deal but managed to line up a new one with another network. *Yay, Waylon.*

As each day passes, I wonder if I'll ever see Chelsea again. She was a good kid. And it felt great to have someone to share my journey. I felt a little less lonely.

It's weird how loneliness works. You're alone long enough, and you start to forget what it feels like to be forsaken. You grow accustomed. But then when you meet someone you connect with and remember what it's like to be human. Then when they're gone, you remember what it means to be truly alone.

I try not to take it personally that Chelsea hasn't come to see me. After all, she's back among the living. Maybe she could only astral travel, or whatever it was she was doing, while in a coma.

I'd call her, but the family changed all of their numbers after the initial surge of publicity surrounding Chelsea coming out of her coma.

I suppose if I tried hard enough I could remember Waylon's number, but I'm not sure what I'd say even if I got through, especially today as a 60-year-old dude. "Hey, I'm trying to reach your client's teenage daughter."

Yeah, that would go over like a lead balloon.

I'm a solo ghost again.

∾

IT's my final job of the day.

I'm sitting outside a grocery store waiting on a little old lady who asked me if I'd mind "waiting just a minute" while she ran in to get something.

I told her no problem.

That was fifteen minutes ago.

Did she stiff me, and flee out the back door? Or maybe she's wandering the aisles suffering from dementia with no idea where she is.

I'm debating whether to go in the store and look for her or leave.

I'm not sure of the protocol. Worse comes to worst, I'm out fifteen bucks and will maybe get a reprimand from my bosses.

I decide to surf the web on my host's phone to kill some time. If I'm gonna wait, I may as well check for any news on the Caldwells before calling it a night.

I usually see the same stories when I search Chelsea Caldwell, but tonight there's a new one at the top of the results, a story published an hour ago.

∽

MIRACLE COMA SURVIVOR Chelsea Caldwell Goes Missing; Teacher Affair To Blame?

∽

WHAT?

I thumb through the story. From the scant information, it appears that Chelsea went out for a walk yesterday afternoon and never came home.

The story then delves into accusations that she was having an affair with Carla. *So much for keeping a lid on that story!* The real shocker is that Carla Valencia is *also* missing.

"Holy shit, they ran off together!" I say, not sure if I'm disappointed or happy for them.

Suddenly, I sense somebody in my back seat.

I turn, expecting to see the old lady to have slipped into the car while I was distracted by this shocker of a story.

But it isn't her.

"Chelsea?" I say, not even sure, as the thing in my back seat is like a fading hologram, jittery with static.

"Ella?" she says, her voice staticky.

"Yes," I say. "Where are you?"

"They took me, Ella."

"Who took you?"

"Some people in a van. They pulled up beside me, put a bag over my head, and took— "

And like that, she's gone.

"Ella?"

She crackles back to life, visually and audibly.

"Where are you?"

"I don't know. It's someplace big. I think I'm … underground. They put me in a coma or something, Ella."

"What?"

"I think they put me in a coma. And I'm not alone."

"What do you mean?"

"There's a whole room of people just like me, all of them in these chambers. And I heard — "

She's gone again.

Shit!

Who the hell took her? Why? And why do they have a room full of people in comas? Why is this happening to her? What did she ever do to deserve this?

I remember the static in the hospital.

Am I picking up on how The Collectors communicate?

Were they looking for Chelsea? And if so, why?

I don't remember the assassin saying The Collectors used vans. This is something different.

But what?

I need to find out where she is.

I need to find her.

I need to save her.

Suddenly, she's back, in the front seat now, clearer than before.

She looks at me as if she can see me better, too.

I can see that she's crying.

"Did you hear me?" she asks.

"You cut out. What did you say?"

"I heard them saying your name, Ella."

"What?"

"I think these are the people looking for you. And they've got me, Ella. I'm scared."

My mind is filled with a helpless panic. I want to save her, but how? I feel blinded by the things I don't know. I look down as if my hands in my lap will hold some answers.

"I'll figure something out," I promise, even though I don't have the first clue how I can fulfill that vow. "You hear me, Chelsea? I will find you."

But she doesn't answer.

She's gone.

The story continues...

If you enjoyed reading *The Collectors* and want to read more, the story continues in *Deviant*, Book Four in the *Karma Police* series.

Start reading Deviant today

A Quick Favor...

If you enjoyed this book, please take a moment to write a short review on your favorite online bookstore so other readers can enjoy it, too.

Thanks so much!

About the Authors

Sean Platt is an entrepreneur and founder of Sterling & Stone, where he makes stories with his partners, Johnny B. Truant, and David W. Wright, and a family of storytellers.

Sean is the bestselling author of over 10 million words' worth of books, including the Yesterday's Gone and Invasion series. Sean is also co-author of the indie publishing cornerstone, Write. Publish. Repeat. and co-host of the Story Studio Podcast.

Originally from Long Beach, California, Sean now lives in Austin, Texas with his wife and two children. He has more than his share of nose.

David W. Wright is the co-author of edge-of-your seat thrillers including the best-selling post-apocalyptic series *Yesterday's Gone,* the paranoid sci-fi *WhiteSpace* series, and the vigilante series, *No Justice*, as well as standalone thrillers *12*, and *Crash* which was recently optioned for a movie.

David is an accomplished, though intermittent, cartoonist who lives in [LOCATION REDACTED] with his wife and son [NAMES REDACTED.]

He is not at all paranoid.

He is "the grumpy one" on the *The Story Studio Podcast* with fellow Sterling and Stone founders, Sean Platt and Johnny B. Truant.

David writes about books, TV shows, movies, and

video games he enjoys; his struggles with anxiety and OCD; writing; and posts the occasional drawing at his personal blog at davidwwright.com

You can email him at david@sterlingandstone.net

We swear, he almost never bites. Unless you feed him after midnight.

For a full list of his most recent books visit sterlingand-stone.net.

Also By Sean Platt

The Dead World Series

Dead Zero

Dead City

Dead Nation

Dead Planet

Empty Nest

The Beam Series

The Beam Season One

The Beam Season Two

The Beam Season Three

Robot Proletariat Series

En3my

Robot Proletariat

The Infinite Loop

The Hard Reset

Cascade Failure

Reboot

The Tomorrow Gene Series

Null Identity

The Tomorrow Gene

The Tomorrow Clone

The Eden Experiment

Karma Police Series

Jumper

Karma Police

The Collectors

Deviant

The Fall

Homecoming

Yesterday's Gone

October's Gone

Yesterday's Gone Season One

Yesterday's Gone Season Two

Yesterday's Gone Season Three

Yesterday's Gone Season Four

Yesterday's Gone Season Five

Yesterday's Gone Season Six

Tomorrow's Gone

Tomorrow's Gone Season One

Tomorrow's Gone Season Two

Tomorrow's Gone Season Three

Available Darkness

Darkness Itself

Available Darkness Book One

Available Darkness Book Two

Available Darkness Book Three

Also By David W. Wright

Cold Vengeance

Cold Vengeance

Cold Reckoning

Hidden Justice

Hidden Justice

Hidden Honor

Hidden Shame

Hidden Virtue

No Justice

No Justice

No Escape

No Hope

No Return

No Stopping

No Fear

Karma Police

Jumper

Karma Police

The Collectors

Deviant

The Fall

Homecoming

Yesterday's Gone

October's Gone

Yesterday's Gone Season One

Yesterday's Gone Season Two

Yesterday's Gone Season Three

Yesterday's Gone Season Four

Yesterday's Gone Season Five

Yesterday's Gone Season Six

Tomorrow's Gone

Tomorrow's Gone Season One

Tomorrow's Gone Season Two

Tomorrow's Gone Season Three

Available Darkness

Darkness Itself

Available Darkness Book One

Available Darkness Book Two

Available Darkness Book Three

WhiteSpace

WhiteSpace Season One

WhiteSpace Season Two

WhiteSpace Season Three

Stand Alone Novels